Meghan's w...
several times ...
wasn't the hair...
propositioned ...
focus up from the button fly of a pair of well-worn jeans.

Her gaze continued up, past a slim waist to a broad chest, beyond a set of wide shoulders until her eyes found his ruggedly handsome face. He was perfect. Absolutely perfect. Tall, dark and fabulous, this bad boy had walked straight out of her erotic fantasies.

"I didn't know it was that kind of resort," he said, grinning. "Usually I have to ask before I get rejected."

The rough timbre of his voice sent a shiver down her spine. "Um, I thought you were someone else."

His smile widened in amusement...and interest? "You mean you *do* want to have sex?"

Meghan didn't know how to respond to his teasing. This guy was too hot. Thinking about her plans to indulge in a no-strings affair with a stranger, she suddenly wasn't so sure she could go through with it. Then he smiled, radiating dark sensuality and dangerous allure.

Then again, she thought. What red-blooded woman could resist?

Blaze™

Dear Reader,

Can you imagine a perfect lover, a man who somehow
knows your secret desires? Can you imagine giving in to
sensual impulses and living out your sexy fantasies?

Meghan Foster wants to have a wildly passionate affair, like the
ones she writes about in her diary. Alex Worth is the kind of guy
fantasies are created for. But the ideal man isn't always what he
seems. Especially when he's using Meghan's own imagination to
seduce her...

I'm thrilled to be writing for Blaze, a line I've enjoyed since its
launch a year and a half ago. These books have brought me
countless hours of sensual reading pleasure. I hope you get as
much enjoyment from reading about Alex and Meghan's sexual
adventures as I did coming up with them.

The journey to publication is often a long and frustrating one.
To find out how I got here, and to see where I'm going, visit
my Web site at www.miazachary.com. Follow your dreams. You
never know where they might take you.

I wish you joy.

Mia Zachary

P.S. While you're online, be sure to check out www.tryblaze.com.

RED SHOES &
A DIARY

Mia Zachary

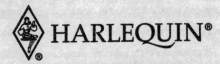

TORONTO • NEW YORK • LONDON
AMSTERDAM • PARIS • SYDNEY • HAMBURG
STOCKHOLM • ATHENS • TOKYO • MILAN • MADRID
PRAGUE • WARSAW • BUDAPEST • AUCKLAND

With love to Mom, who always believed,
and to Heather, who was always there.

I'm deeply grateful to my wonderful editor, Brenda Chin, for
taking a chance and for hating my cruise ship. Special thanks to
my critique partners, Kelly Young and Deanna Lilly, and to all
my friends at www.cataromance.com.

ISBN 0-373-79087-2

RED SHOES & A DIARY

Copyright © 2003 by Mika Boblitz.

Visit us at www.eHarlequin.com

Printed in U.S.A.

Monday, July 14

What will it be like to have a physical encounter with a stranger? To give myself over to sexual exploration and shed my inhibitions?

On these pages, as "Elise," my other self, I've been wild and sensual, daring and seductive. I've fantasized about a tall, dark-haired lover who makes me feel sexy, desirable, feminine. I've dreamed of taking chances, letting go.

With the last entry of this diary comes a new beginning. What will it be like to find a lover and say, "Take me, I'm yours"?

1

ALEX WORTH STRODE down the fancy marbled hallway, looking for his room—his "suite." He never thought a guy like him would be staying in a place like the Cayo Sueño Resort. Finally, an undercover assignment with perks.

His conscience spoke loudly in his head. *Remember how you got here. Don't forget what's at stake.*

He ignored the stab of guilt and kept walking. There, on the left. Room—*Suite* 809. He disengaged the lock and swung the door open. The first thing he noticed was a pair of sandals in front of the couch. The cherry-red high heels had "seduce me" written all over them.

Alex glanced at his magnetic hotel card key and then checked it against the door number. He was in the right place. He looked back over at the sexy sandals. Talk about service. The hotel room came with a woman.

"Hello?"

He listened intently for any sound of movement. Nothing.

After setting his carry-all in the foyer, he slammed the door shut as a warning.

Still no answer. The thick carpet muffled his steps as he moved farther into the suite. He called out again, his voice echoing off the pale papered walls.

"Hello? Anyone here?"

He poked his head into the bathroom. No woman. Just a makeup bag on the vanity and a used towel hanging on the shower rod. The living room was empty, too, except for the lingering scent of perfume. Something floral, but somehow smoky...

A lace-edged bra and matching panties were carefully arranged on the couch cushion. Alex smirked. Who was this woman? The bright red lingerie had been laid out precisely, like she'd wanted to see how they'd look on her body. He picked up the bra, trying to imagine the breasts that fit into it. The satin fabric felt slippery between his fingers and it wasn't hard to picture a hot babe who was equally slick.

He dropped the bra back on the couch, scooped the sandals off the floor and headed for the other room. Maybe the woman was lounging on the bed silently waiting for him.

Nope. No such luck. What the hell was going on? How did she get into his suite, and more importantly, where was she now?

Two small suitcases sat against the wall beside the closet. He set the shoes down and flipped one of the luggage tags around. Apparently Meghan Elise Foster was visiting Florida from Baltimore, Maryland. He had a name now, but her reason for being here was still a mystery.

He'd been invited to Cayo Sueño by Rogelio Braga, his connection in the Miami cartel. Braga was supposed to introduce him to the infamous Frankie Ramos. So Alex couldn't trust anything about this trip, not even bright red panties that begged, "touch me." Too many good agents had been compromised in situations just like this.

A third suitcase lay open on the bed. It was half full, as if she'd been interrupted. He didn't hesitate over rummaging through the contents. He'd worked undercover too long to let a little issue like privacy stop him. He had to know who this woman was.

The "touch me" panties and "seduce me" sandals didn't go with the clothes laid out on the bed. Quality, with recognizable labels, but kind of plain. The skirts were long, the necklines high and everything was a solid color, not a stripe or pattern in sight.

On the other hand, the underwear couldn't have been hotter. He recognized it from his ex-wife's catalogues that still came to the house. Bright floral demi bras, satin tap pants and lace camisoles spilled from the suitcase. Most of the stuff still had price tags attached.

Weird. Maybe Ms. Foster was going through some kind of identity crisis—something he could easily relate to. Still, this whole thing was making him uneasy. He'd turned to leave when he noticed a hardbound book on the window seat. It looked like an address book or a calendar.

Curious, he went over to check it out. Guessing from the handwritten paragraphs on the open page, he'd found Ms. Foster's journal. He focused on the actual words and his brows shot up in surprise. Whoa.

Suddenly he appears, glorious in his nakedness. Tall and strong and beautiful, my fantasy lover stands beside me under the waterfall. He raises his arms to me and the bright sun lights the water droplets rolling down his magnificent body. He moves toward me, offers himself to me. No ges-

ture could be more flattering, more seductive, than
seeing the rigid proof that I am desired.

As the image burned itself into Alex's brain, the effect was hard and immediate. His skin felt hot, his chest
tight, as his pulse accelerated. He clapped the book shut
before tossing it back onto the window seat. It slipped
off the edge, pages flapping, and fell to the floor. He
stared at the blue paisley cover for a second, struggling
with his conscience.

Arousal won. He rifled the pages until he found the
waterfall entry again.

He wraps his arms around me, lifts me off my
feet, all the while plundering my mouth with his
tongue. Our bodies join as he lowers me onto him.
I cry out from the sheer intensity of the pleasure
as he begins to rock his hips. Mating beneath the
cascade, he lifts me repeatedly, my body sliding,
his thrusting—

Knock knock knock.

Startled, Alex snapped the journal shut. In the space
of a breath he went on alert, adrenaline pumping into
his system. It couldn't be Ms. Foster. She didn't have
to knock. Only two people knew for certain he was
here—one a friend, the other a target. And his partner
wasn't due to arrive until later.

He reached around for the gun in the waistband of
his jeans. Shit. His Beretta was back in Miami with his
badge and his real ID. The finance geek he was im-
personating wouldn't be armed. He had to get himself
together—fast.

His name was "Nicholas Alexander." He owned a small brokerage firm in Coral Gables. He was here to discuss ways of moving the cartel's money out of the country.

Show time.

Grabbing the knob, he closed his eyes, willing his rapid pulse to slow. He remembered the muzzle flash. A sharp crack of sound. Pain. His eyes flew open. "Nick" swallowed hard and answered the door.

A bellman stood in the entrance, a professional smile on his face. "Mr. Alexander? I have a delivery for you, sir."

Alex controlled his expression, gave away none of his relief. He transferred the small book he still held into his right hand. "Do I need to sign anything?"

"No, sir. This came from within the resort." The young man handed over a bottle of champagne and bid him a good afternoon.

Back in the living room, he put the bottle and the note that came with it on the coffee table. No problem. Just a delivery. He didn't have to face Braga yet. He could relax.

Too bad his body didn't respond as fast as his brain.

Sinking heavily onto the sofa, he rested his elbows on his knees and drew in a shaky breath. He swiped his palms up and down his face, irritated to discover beads of sweat around his hairline. The panic attacks were coming too often.

Deep unhappiness, resentment and frustration welled up inside him, making his eyes sting. The nausea slowly dissipated, but its aftereffect gnawed at his confidence. He brushed the fingers of his left hand over the scar on his temple.

I don't know what the hell I'm doing anymore.

He'd spent the past eight years in the Drug Enforcement Agency, three and a half of those with the Special Operations Division, a joint national task force of agents, prosecutors and analysts from the DEA, FBI and U.S. Customs Service. Alex considered himself one of the best agents the SOD had. He was the first one through the door, the first one to volunteer for assignments. The job had always been enough— Hell, it was everything until six weeks ago.

The meeting in Overtown had gone south when an informant double-crossed the team. She was killed in the ensuing gunfire and his partner's cover was blown. "Nick" had inadvertently saved Rogelio Braga's life, but landed in the hospital with a bullet graze on his forehead.

Over the past month, his mild anxiety had escalated to a sickening panic. Post-Traumatic Stress Disorder. The DEA psychologist had patiently explained it. Most law enforcement personnel exhibited some symptoms following a traumatic stressor. Alex had silently glared through the mandatory therapy.

PTSD, my ass. He just had trouble sleeping, that was all.

After successfully infiltrating the cartel, he was under a lot of pressure to close the case. As the stakes increased, so did the dread of being shot in the face again. He hated this…weakness. And he was starting to hate this job.

He picked up the champagne and inspected the label before reading the note. "Alexander. Welcome to Cayo Sueño. I hope you enjoy my little gift. I'm sure you will put it to good use. Braga."

A gift, huh? The smoky floral perfume lingering in the room tickled his nostrils. He needed to track down Meghan Foster and figure out whether she was here by accident or by design. Either way, he couldn't wait to see how she looked wearing those cherry-red sandals.

"I JUST HAD sex on the beach. Wanna try it?"

A bony elbow nudged Meghan Foster in the ribs. She turned until she was cleavage to face with the hairiest man she'd ever seen. The fur on his chin and torso more than compensated for the lack of a single strand on his head.

"Excuse me?" She backed up against the rail of the pool deck, suppressing the urge to cross her arms over her breasts.

"It's a joke. Ya know, Sex on the Beach. The drink?" He raised his umbrella-laden glass to indicate the pink liquid inside. "So, how 'bout it? We could have 'Sex' together."

Meghan shuddered at the image of this hairy gnome wearing nothing but sand and a gap-toothed smile. "Um, no. I think not."

"Ya don't know what yer missing, girlie."

"I do, actually."

The gnome shrugged his fuzzy shoulders and went off to accost someone else.

Quite a few of her diary fantasies involved water. In fact, she'd written several versions of the famous scene in the movie *From Here to Eternity.* But if another man ever suggested making love in the surf, he'd better be younger, taller and better-looking.

A steel band played for the welcome reception and her hips swayed to the beat of the Calypso tune. Looking around, she couldn't believe the crowd. The party had turned into good-natured chaos, overflowing from the veranda onto the sundeck above the main pool.

Pushing her glasses into place, Meghan squinted against the glare from the aquamarine water. Pale gray clouds flirted with the late afternoon sun, but did little to dispel the heat. She was really sorry she'd chosen this outfit. The silk blouse clung to her skin and her linen walking shorts felt too thick and heavy. She swallowed the last mouthful of cola from her crystal tumbler and set it on the rail.

Angling her head from side to side, she searched the crowd for her sister. Julie was the Cayo Sueño entertainment director. She and Mom had saved up to surprise Meghan with this much-needed holiday. Mom had even told her *not* to behave herself.

The memory made her smile. She had absolutely no intention of being a good girl. A week on Dream Key was exactly what she needed to start her new life and she wasn't going to waste a single moment. Tilting her face toward the Florida sun, she imagined the humid air smelled hot, spicy and a little dangerous.

That's going to be me—hot, spicy and dangerous.

Uptight. Cold. Boring. Rob's words echoed nastily in her mind. He'd flung the insults at her the day she'd found the crotchless panties. She'd never in her life worn crotchless panties.

How dumb could one person be? When Rob had told her he was working late, she'd believed him. When he'd said he had to go out of town on business, she'd still believed him. And the whole time he'd been boinking that silicone-enhanced blonde at the office.

He hadn't even bothered to deny he was cheating, and that hurt worse than the affair itself.

Rob blamed Meghan for the affair, accusing her of being too inexperienced and withdrawn to satisfy him. He'd found a "real" woman who was sexy and adventurous and sophisticated—all of the things that she wasn't. All of the things she couldn't be—except in her secret diary.

The betrayal had left her emotionally shattered and totally unsure of her appeal as a woman. She'd known something was missing in their relationship. When they'd had sex, part of her had held back from fully giving and accepting pleasure— Meghan shoved the memory aside, determined to move on. The past couldn't be undone, no matter how hard she wished.

What she needed was an affair of her own. The kind of no-strings, no-regrets sexual encounter she had only written and dreamed about. This week, she was finally going to live a little, have fun, go wild. She was going to be a Sex Goddess in Training. Once she found the right guy—

An elbow knocked into her ribs again. She huffed out an impatient sigh, expecting to see the hairy little gnome again. She whirled to confront him, tilting her head down as she spoke.

"Listen. I don't want to have sex...." The words faded into silence. She blinked several times as her cheeks started to flame. Definitely not the gnome. Slowly, she pulled her focus up from the button fly of a pair of well-worn jeans.

Her gaze continued up, way up, past a slim waist to a broad chest covered by a blue-and-yellow floral shirt. She looked beyond muscular arms to a set of wide shoulders until her eyes found the ruggedly handsome face. Seeing the sable hair tousled over his forehead, her fingers itched to test the silkiness of those unruly strands. It looked like he hadn't shaved his short, dark whiskers in days.

Omigod. A tiny gold hoop sparkled in his left ear-lobe!

The modern-day pirate arched one eyebrow. That's when she noticed a thin groove that ended at his hairline. Startled, she dropped her gaze to his mouth. Big mistake. He had a wide mouth with full, totally kissable lips. They parted in a dazzling display of even, white teeth. The friendly-yet-sexy grin sent a wave of lust rushing though her.

He was perfect. Absolutely perfect. Tall, dark and fabulous, this bad boy had walked straight out of her erotic fantasies. She saw her own gaping reflection in the mirrored sunglasses hiding his eyes and closed her mouth.

"Didn't know it was that kind of resort. Usually I have to ask before I get rejected."

The rough timbre of his voice sent a shiver down her spine. Who would be crazy enough to reject him? Meghan pushed her eyeglasses back onto her nose. This guy was just too incredible to be real.

"Um, I thought you were someone else."

His smile widened in amusement...and interest? "You mean, you do want to have sex?"

"Not with the gnome. I mean— Oh, never mind." His rumbling chuckle turned her on even more.

Now would be a great time for a dignified exit, but she was frozen in place. No, not frozen. This guy was too hot. She continued to stare at her fantasy come to life. Faced with the reality of seducing a stranger, she wasn't sure she could go through with it. Then he smiled again, radiating dark sensuality and a dangerous allure.

What Sex Goddess in Training could resist?

2

He is everything I ever wanted in a man, all that I've dreamed of. When I see him, there is a primitive recognition. Ours eyes meet, our souls collide.

"You're not what I expected."

"Pardon?" Meghan blinked and focused on the pirate instead of her runaway pheromones.

"Um, I meant you're kind of overdressed for a beachside resort." His mouth curved into an odd smile. "Nice shoes."

She glanced down at the high-heeled white sandals that went with her walking shorts. "I guess I haven't gotten into vacation mode yet."

With a tip of his head, he indicated the crowd of people around them. "This is some party, huh?"

"It just got a lot better." Was she flirting? She was flirting. Cool.

His smile widened at the inadvertent compliment and he stood a little taller, if that were possible. "I was thinking the same thing."

Meghan dropped her gaze, not believing him. This guy was sending out signals that had her completely off-balance. She fidgeted, twirling the gold bracelet around her wrist. "So, do you come here often?"

"Never been to this resort before, but I spend a lot of time in Key West."

"What do you do?"

"I'm a broker."

She glanced at his shirt. A blind man could see that bold, gaudy pattern a mile away. "Forgive the observation, but it's hard to picture you calling orders down to the trading floor."

"Working vacations are always casual. What about you?"

Someone jostled him from behind. As he turned to look, he took an unconscious step toward her. His right hand bumped her breast and a shock of awareness zinged along her nerve endings. She gasped and he swung around, looking at her curiously.

Wow. If she reacted like this to an accidental fondle, she wasn't sure she could handle a deliberate one. Reeling from the thrill of his unexpected touch, it took a second to remember his question.

"Oh, um. For the past few years I've been working as a paralegal."

"That's a legal assistant, right?"

"Yes. I did most of the work for a trial, like filing documents with the court, interviewing witnesses and preparing evidence." Meghan realized she was babbling. She smoothed a damp palm over her hair and cleared her throat. "Anyway, I'm starting at University of Miami Law this fall."

"So you're going to be an attorney." The corners of his mouth angled into a smirk. "Did you hear they're using lawyers in lab experiments now? Apparently there are some things even rats won't do.''

"Gee, I never heard that one before.'' She rolled her eyes and laughed along with him. "I'm going into civil law, not criminal. I want to do mediation and binding arbitration.''

"I guess this is your last vacation for a while.'' He tipped his beer bottle toward her in salute. "Here's hoping it's a memorable one.''

She felt another wave of heat, and not just in her cheeks. His voice was low and smooth, as sensuous as the rasp of bodies sliding over satin sheets... The sound of laughter and applause brought her back to the present.

"Want to see what's going on?'' Her pirate gallantly offered her his arm, placing her hand in the crook of his elbow. His skin felt warm, the dark hairs silky. Her fingertips tingled at the point of contact, sending a tremor along her nerves.

He forged a path to the pool side of the deck, made space near the railing and maneuvered her to stand in front of him. His body heat penetrated her back and she had a crazy urge to rub her tush against his zipper.

Very subtly, she angled her head to the side. Casting a glance over one shoulder, Meghan studied her fantasy man. She mentally stripped off his garish shirt and tight jeans. His body would be perfect—she just knew it. Lean, hard, athletic. Hard.

If she felt the stirrings of lust, this damp and quivering desire, then she couldn't be frigid. Her reaction to this gorgeous guy proved that she was a normal, healthy woman.

He must have sensed her ogling him, because he

looked down and grinned knowingly. Busted. With a hot blush and a quiet sigh, she turned her attention to the makeshift stage below.

The staff at Cayo Sueño introduced themselves. She listened absently to the various names, origins and job titles.

"—happy to plan your exercise and workout schedule—"

"—adventures await, so stop on by the tour desk—"

"—the fairway at the Key West Golf Club—"

She smiled when Julie grabbed the microphone. The crisp white uniform flattered her sister's pretty bronze face and showed off her great figure. Jules enthusiastically related the activities available both on and off the island.

"Personally, I don't think seven days is long enough to enjoy everything we have to offer!"

"Why do I suddenly feel like I'm on a cruise ship?" The pirate murmured the comment, his breath tickling her ear.

She laughed and tilted her face to look up at him. "Cross your fingers we don't have to play shuffleboard."

He seemed to hold her gaze, but she couldn't be sure. She wanted him to take off the sunglasses so she could see his eyes. Would they be green, like the man in her fantasies? *Please let them be green.*

Jules briefly mentioned the pre-Columbian ruins on the northeast side of the island. She went on to list some of the tours available in Key West, fifteen minutes away, as well as trips to the Lower Keys and the Dry Tortugas National Park. After wishing everyone a fabulous vacation, she said, "Oh, one last thing while I've got everybody's attention. The woman on the upper deck in the beige blouse and white shorts is my sister.''

Startled, Meghan tore her gaze away from the pirate to gape down at Julie, who waved wildly in her direction. It seemed a hundred pairs of eyes turned to stare. Her stomach clutched in dread and she stood motionless in the spotlight of sudden attention.

"It's Meghan's first vacation in two years and her first ever visit to Cayo Sueño. I just know you guys are going to make sure she has some fun this week. Thanks!"

For the millionth time in her life, she wished she were an only child. "Julie Anne Foster, I'm going to kill you."

"Bad idea to announce that in front of witnesses. They tend to remember it when the body is found."

She turned in the circle of his arm where he rested his hand on the railing. Despite her embarrassment, excitement caught fire in her belly. She was practically in his embrace. All she had to do was lean her head back to kiss him.

"This isn't funny. One of these guys could be a deranged ax-murdering rapist. Now, no thanks to my meddling sister, he knows my name."

"Al—" His voice hitched, then he straightened and offered his hand. "Nick. Nicholas Alexander. I'm not an ax murderer. I swear."

She snickered in appreciation of the joke and reached out. When his large palm enveloped her hand, the softness of his skin surprised her. "Nice to meet you, Nick."

He finally peeled his sunglasses off and she saw his

eyes for the first time. Omigod. They were the light green of spring leaves with long dark lashes. Even better than her fantasy man's.

He continued to clasp her fingers, tilting his head as if studying her. "And you're Meghan Elise Foster from Baltimore."

How did he know all that? Taken aback by the odd tone of his voice, she slipped her hand away. "Yes, I am."

He stared at her intently, as if he could see into her soul. No one had ever looked at her so…thoroughly. She could lose herself in his eyes. And in the slow, sexy grin unfolding on his face.

"In that case, you've got real nice underwear."

"Excuse me?" She spread one hand over her chest, in case he could somehow see her bra.

His tone was too intimate, his expression too knowing, as he eyed her up and down. "The red lacy ones. Very sexy."

How could he have seen her underwear? Only the sales clerk had seen her brand-new underwear. "What in the world are you talking about?"

"You left them draped on my couch."

"*Your* sofa?"

"Looks like you checked into my suite by mistake. Not that I mind sharing. But I thought you'd want to know."

"There must be some mistake." She dug the magnetic card key out of her tote bag and held it up for him to see. "I have suite number 809."

"Nope. It's upside-down." His warm fingers curled over her wrist, then turned her hand until the card faced the opposite way. "You have room number 608. 809 is mine."

Well, that explained the underwear. Not wanting to believe the awkwardness of the situation, she drew her brows together in confusion. "But this key fits the lock to that suite."

"Then I'll take a rain check on seeing you wear those red, lacy panties." He winked at her, his arrogant reply tempered by a dash of charm and a seductive smile.

The breath hitched in her throat and her mouth suddenly went dry. *The cold sting of rain hit Elise's bare skin as his hot body lowered onto hers...* Swallowing hard, Meghan concentrated on the problem at hand. Adopting a brisk manner, she shrugged the tote bag into place on her shoulder. "Let's go check with the front desk, shall we?"

They joined the group of irritated guests already at the hotel's reservation desk. The manager apologized to everyone for the apparent malfunction of the key coder. The computer had failed to change the access numbers upon checkout and several rooms were double assigned before the mistake was discovered.

Fifteen minutes later, Meghan stood in the open doorway of suite 809 with Nick and a security guard. She couldn't believe this. "Are you certain this is necessary, Mr. Brooks?"

"You asked me that four times, ma'am. And for the fifth time, I'm tellin' you it's hotel policy not to let no one into another room unescorted."

Nick tried to reason with the man. "She's not going to steal anything. Most of the things in there are hers anyway."

"Hotel policy—"

"She's not unescorted. I'm standing right here. You don't have to make her feel like a criminal." He turned to let his eyes roam over her figure. "Besides, if she does try anything, I'm pretty sure I can take her."

Oh, he could take her all right. And she wouldn't resist at all. Temptation dared her to grab the resort bathrobe and bolt just for the chance to wrestle against his long, lean body.

The security guard finally gave in, apparently having taken all the grief he was going to. "Fine, sir. Don't come yellin' for me if you got stuff missing."

When the door closed behind them, Meghan found herself alone with the sexiest man on the face of the earth. Alone with the sexiest man and her own raging hormones. She had to clear her throat before she could speak. "Thank you. I was beginning to think he planned to frisk me."

"Allow me." He wiggled his brows and placed one hand on the wall behind her head. "Are you concealing anything? Stolen pillow mints? Pilfered matchbooks?"

His eyes challenged her while his other hand reached out. She held his stare with effort when he stroked his fingertips down her bare arm. Butterflies trembled in her stomach and she gasped softly when he lowered his head.

Omigod. He's going to kiss me.

She flattened a palm against his chest to stop him. Heat radiated through the bright fabric and her pulse accelerated to match the beating of his heart. Then the sensual light went out of his eyes, replaced by something akin to confusion.

Did he think she was a tease? She wanted to play

fast and loose this week, she really did. Just not quite so soon. If she let him keep advancing, they might end up doing it right here on the floor. Hmm. Actually… No, not yet.

Nick looked down at her hand, then back into her eyes. The intimacy of the touch unsettled her and she snatched her fingers away. *Uptight. Inexperienced.* Embarrassed.

"The only contraband I have is the soap and the herbal shampoo." Ducking under his extended arm, she darted toward the bedroom to repack.

"Speaking of things that ought to be illegal…"

Hearing the smoky familiarity in his tone, she turned back in time to see him come out of the living room. Her brows furrowed in curiosity, then shot up in alarm. Would the humiliation of this day never end?

"Guess you'll be needing these back." Nick held out one sculpted arm, dangling her bra and panties from his hand. He casually stroked his thumb over her intimate wear.

His fingers grazed the edge of Elise's panties, tickling the sensitive skin along her inner thigh, before sliding inside… Meghan blinked, tried to refocus. The corner of Nick's mouth quirked and the look in his eyes was pure mischief, as if he suspected her reaction and dared her to come closer to the source.

Okay. She could do this. Lifting her chin, she threw back her shoulders and walked toward him. He skimmed his fingers across her palm when he returned her lingerie. Another hot current passed between them.

A rush of anxiety immediately followed.

What was *she* doing flirting with a guy like Nick? He could have any woman he wanted. So what mental disorder made her think he'd waste time on her? Loneliness and longing twisted her heart, overwhelmed her. She was boring, she was frigid—she was doing it again.

Meghan slammed the self-doubt aside, concentrated instead on her mission. The plan was to find an attractive man and then entice him into spending the next week indulging in decadent pleasures. Well, she'd found a guy and he was perfect. Nick was everything she imagined the fantasy lover in her diary to be. His dangerously compelling gaze made her yearn for wild excitement and erotic adventure.

Ask him.

She cleared her throat and prepared to inject a sensuous note into her voice. Then she hesitated, not yet braced for rejection, unwilling to make herself vulnerable. No matter how much she wanted to live out her fantasies, things were moving too fast. She should at least make sure he wasn't an ax murderer before she tried to take him to bed.

Meghan flicked her gaze away and slid the garments out of his hand. She couldn't bear to meet his eye and see his reaction to her failed attempt at seduction. "Thank you very much."

"My pleasure." His rich voice held more than a hint of innuendo. "You know, you didn't strike me as the red lace type."

She pressed her lips together and shoved her glasses back onto her nose. Maybe she wasn't a Sex Goddess yet, but Elise sure was. Red lace underwear and enough attitude to bring any man to his knees. Including Nick.

"You don't know me well enough to decide what type I am." Her voice quavered despite her effort to sound confident. She turned on her heel and went into the bedroom. After dropping her tote bag, she hauled open the nearest suitcase and shoved the lingerie inside.

Old heartache welled up inside her, fueled by memories of shyness and humiliation, fanned by self-doubt and fear. She never seemed to fit in anywhere, not even in her own skin.

ALEX WATCHED the fire die out, watched Meghan pull into herself. He was more intrigued than ever. The lady was a walking contradiction. Those journal entries were hot enough to ignite the pages. But now she acted like she wanted to be invisible.

How in the hell could this be the same woman?

Leaning one hip against the dresser, he crossed his arms over his chest and studied her. Meghan Elise Foster from Baltimore wasn't at all what he'd expected. The description he'd gotten from housekeeping didn't do her justice.

Short, brown curls framed an interesting face. Behind the wire-rimmed glasses, her eyes were the color of a good single-malt scotch. Warm and sparkling with intelligence. Her golden skin was flawless, highlighted by the sweet flush coloring her cheeks. She had freckles on her nose and a stubborn set to her chin.

Her small, but perfectly formed breasts would fit nicely in the palms of his hands. She had round hips, a great butt and her shapely legs went on forever. He was dying to find out how they'd feel wrapped around his waist.

Moving gracefully around the room, she was doing her best to pretend he wasn't there. But the frequent glances from under her lashes gave her away. Alex grinned. She was trying way too hard to ignore him. Damned if he would let her. He drifted closer, narrowing the space between them.

"Need any help?"

"I can manage, thank you."

She gathered her cotton T-shirts, linen shorts, and plain black swimsuit out of the dresser. The neatly folded clothing was just as neatly repacked into the suitcase. She brushed past him, unnecessarily close, and her exotic scent filled his senses. Like getting socked in the gut without warning.

"What's your perfume called?"

She looked over, startled by the question. "It's body oil, actually. Calendula flower."

"It suits you."

"Oh, really. How so?" Wary curiosity laced her tone.

He cocked his head to one side, assessing what he'd learned about her so far. "Sweet, with an unexpected hint of spice."

She grinned at him, obviously pleased by the description. The shallow dimple added character to an already pretty smile. Alex wanted to feel that mouth all over his body. Lord have mercy, those lush curving lips could get a man into serious trouble.

And "trouble" was just how he thought of her. He had a job to do, had to prove himself to the DEA all over again. He'd been trained to handle every situation with a cool, clear head. He wasn't supposed to feel like this, wasn't supposed to lose control. Her kind of distraction he didn't need.

His body disagreed. Firmly.

When she picked up the cherry-red "seduce me"

sandals, his imagination went into overdrive. He saw her laid out on his bed, wearing the sandals and nothing else, reading her journal to him in that soft husky voice. He shifted to ease the pressure on his zipper.

Alex reached into the open dresser, pulled out a nightgown she'd forgotten in the corner. The white silk whispered through his fingers. He held it up by its thin straps, easily picturing the delicate material against her tawny skin.

"What I said before didn't come out right. I just assumed a classy lady like yourself wore white or pink or cream."

"And so you were right."

He noticed her pulse flutter in her throat as he prowled toward her. "But I'll bet the red lace looks incredible on you."

"Yes, it does."

She held his gaze boldly, like she was testing him instead of the other way around. A wild passion burned through the sadness in her eyes when she looked at him and suddenly he recognized her. She was "Elise," the real woman hiding inside that killer body. No question.

"Why don't you show me?"

"Why don't we leave some things to the imagination? I'm not in the habit of letting strangers see me in my underwear."

"Lady, those teeny scraps of cloth don't have enough room for my imagination."

He'd never reacted to a woman like this before. He wanted to strip away the contradictory layers down to the hot babe hiding inside. Uncovering secrets was his business and he wanted to discover hers, despite his mission and the possibility that she was somehow involved.

Meghan didn't seem like the type to be working for the cartel. Still, he didn't like coincidences. And recent events had taught him about deception. If she worked for Braga, he'd find out soon enough. If not, he'd allow himself the brief pleasure of her company before concentrating on his job.

Alex stood close, deliberately invading her space, brushing his index finger across her lower lip. Her eyes widened and her quick intake of breath was one of the sexiest sounds he'd ever heard. He held her gaze, dared her to look away.

"Spend the night with me. Then we won't be strangers."

3

In fantasies, I can be anyone I want, do anything I please. I can follow my impulses and indulge my wildest desires. Best of all, my fantasies are completely anonymous.

MEGHAN UNPACKED her suitcases for the second time that day. "Well, it's been anything but boring so far."

"What do you mean?" The charms on Julie's bracelet jingled as she flipped her hair over one shoulder.

"First, a gnome propositioned me and you made me into this week's charity case. Then, I had to wrestle my underwear away from a modern-day pirate."

Julie let out a peal of laughter. "A gnome and a pirate? I don't remember including them in our advertising brochure."

"The gnome isn't important." She opened a drawer and laid her lingerie inside. "As for the pirate, he's the gorgeous guy whose suite I checked into by mistake."

"He wasn't wearing your underwear, I hope."

"No, he only fondled it." Instantly, she recalled the sight of her bright red panties draped over Nick's olive skin—and her burning desire to be wearing the lingerie the next time he got his hands on it.

"I can only imagine how my straitlaced big sister must have reacted! What did you say to him?"

Meghan affected a nonchalant tone. Jules was so easy to tease. "I agreed to spend the night with him."

"Excuse me?"

"He asked me to have dinner with him."

"Oh." She sat back in the chair and reached for another piece of the almond-crusted brie. "That's a relief. I thought you meant—"

"I'm planning to take him for a lover."

"Excuse me?" Julie's voice rose to a squeak and she dropped the cheese back onto the tray.

"I said—"

"I heard you." She shook her head, her tone emphatic. "You are not serious."

Meghan planted her hands on both hips and answered with a steely resolve. "I'm quite serious. He's great-looking, charming and very sexy. I think Nick would be a perfect lover."

"You've never taken a wrong step in your entire life. I doubt you'll start now." Julie dismissed the idea with a wave of her hand and picked up her cheese again. "You need a nice, steady guy with a house and a dog, a guy who'll be loyal and dependable."

"Based on that description, I should just get the dog. I'm not looking for a relationship, Jules."

"That's great, except you're not the kind of woman who takes a lover."

"Everyone keeps assuming they know what type of person I am. Did it ever occur to you that you don't know me at all?"

Julie stared at her. "But it's not like you to be impulsive or reckless. For thirteen years, after Dad deserted us, you held our family together. Mom depended on you for everything and you practically raised me, even though we're only two years apart.''

Meghan ignored the bitterness seeping into her gut. The past couldn't be undone, no matter how she wished it could. She kept her tone even when she spoke. "I've always done what other people expected of me, rarely what I wanted to do—"

"I know that, Megs, and I'm sorry. But don't think it goes unappreciated. Mom and I wouldn't have made it without your support."

"Well, now that you've got this great job and Mom is in love again, it's finally my turn to have a life. There's an urgent need building inside me. A need to be reckless and daring, to be swept away into a passionate affair."

"You're a nice girl—"

"I don't want to be a nice girl! I want to be bad." She crossed her arms and raised her chin defiantly. "I'm twenty-seven years old. I've never done anything exciting or unexpected. This week is my chance."

Julie spoke with quiet firmness. "Megs, you wouldn't even know how."

"Is it really so far-fetched to think I could find a boy toy, use his body for my personal pleasure, then walk away with a smile on my face?"

"Yes, it is."

Frustration and resentment stabbed at her. She was getting advice on her love life from her younger sister, who'd not only dated more, but gotten married first. How wrong was that?

"There's so much locked up inside me, Jules. I can't really put it into words. I look at myself in the mirror

and wonder who that woman is and I'm afraid she's
the ice princess Rob described.''

"You're nothing like that, Megs! You're warm and
sweet—''

She walked toward the window, not wanting to see
Julie's reaction as she bared her secret. "Maybe this
seems crazy, but I need to do this. I want to be impulsive and wild. I want to be a real woman who isn't
afraid of her sexuality.''

A woman like Elise.

"I don't think you're crazy, I think you're brave.''
She turned back to see Julie smiling in admiration. "If
this is what you really want, then go for it.''

Meghan grinned in relief. It had been hard to admit
that she wasn't the perfect upstanding older sister after
all. Feeling lighter for having shared her burden, she
reached for the crab quiche on the hors d'oeuvres tray.
Foster women never let emotion interfere with food.

"So, can you turn me into a seductress?'' She'd had
the idea before arriving at Cayo Sueño, but now that
she'd met Nick, she needed a specific plan.

"Of course.'' Julie took the last egg roll. "But not
with the stuff you just took out of those suitcases.''

Meghan studied her reflection in the bedroom mirror.
She could stand to lose ten pounds, but her figure
wasn't bad. Her overall image was classic, professional, conservative—not exactly seductress material.

"I love the underwear, Megs, it's great. But the outer
you needs to reflect the inner you. If you're going to
be a sexpot, you'll have to dress like one.''

"I quit my job, Jules. This isn't the time for me to
spend money on a new wardrobe.''

"I'll lend you some of my clothes. Come by my

cottage before dinner, and I'll do your makeup, too. We're going to make you irresistible and then find the man of your dreams!''

Nick was the man she wanted. Tall, dark and handsome with a dynamic personality and a very nice rear end, he was pure sex in a really ugly shirt. He was so much like her fantasy man it was scary. Well, except for the shirt.

"Okay, let's talk about this fabulous guy." Julie walked into the living room and took out a sheet of the resort's stationery.

Meghan stood beside the chair, tilting her head to see over her shoulder. "What are you doing?"

"I'm making a list of necessary traits for Mr. Fabulous. This way you can narrow down your search."

"I've already made my choice."

"Then, tonight at dinner you can see if Nick qualifies." Julie looked up as she explained. "He's got to be romantic. You know, the gift-for-no-reason and flowers-just-because type."

Meghan didn't really care about this. She just wanted to have great sex. Then again, being pursued and persuaded might be fun, too.

Julie went on. "He's also got to be sensitive, so you feel comfortable exploring new sexual frontiers with him. Most importantly, he's got to be ugly."

"Have you lost your mind?" Leaning over, she tried to grab the pen away. "Nick is not ugly. Far from it."

Julie wrestled the pen back. "According to all the talk shows, an ugly man won't ever cheat. He'll be too grateful a beautiful woman like you deigned to notice him."

Meghan rolled her eyes. "What kind of crazy list are you making?"

"Okay, you can find Mr. Fabulous by yourself."

She picked up the paper. In addition to *romantic* and *sensitive,* Julie had written *adventurous, daring, heroic.* A deep sorrow filled her. It was a description of her late brother-in-law. She looked over at Julie.

"I loved him and I miss him, too, but—"

Her sister met her gaze with a sad smile. "It's all right to say Kyle's name."

Memories of him flooded her mind, along with her own guilt over the way he died. "I'm sorry, Jules. It's just that I'm not looking for a man who chases after danger. Like you said, I need someone I'll be safe with."

"Nobody understands your fears better than me. I'll always be grateful for the times you came over to stay with me. It wasn't easy being married to a cop, living every day in uncertainty, wondering every night if he would come home." Her voice was edged with grief. "But I wouldn't trade a single day we were together, despite how things ended."

"Oh, Jules."

Understanding passed between them as Julie wiped a hand under her eyes. "But, hey, you're not looking for a husband anyway. Come on, let's get back to Mr. Fabulous."

Grateful to change the subject, Meghan took out a fresh sheet of paper. She silently made out a list that included her real wishes, as well as a number of silly qualities guaranteed to make Julie smile again.

"Okay, Mr. Fabulous has to be worldly. I want to be able to discuss current events and world politics."

"You hate politics, and when was the last time you read a newspaper?" Julie tried to grab the paper from her.

Meghan held on and continued as if she hadn't been interrupted. "He also has to be intelligent, sensitive, romantic, successful, virile, sexy and prompt."

"Prompt? Give me a break. Come on, admit it. All you really want is a guy who (a)looks like a fashion model and (b)makes love like a porn star."

They both dissolved into peals of laughter. After catching her breath, Julie glanced at her watch and winced. "I've got to get back to work. I'm hosting a party by the Cascade Pool tonight and there's still a lot to do."

Meghan wrapped both arms around her sister in a fierce hug. "Thank you again. I really appreciate everything you've done for me."

"I'm so glad you're here. You're going to have a great week!" Julie kissed her cheek. "Hey, why don't you come to the party? It's the perfect place to look for Mr. Fabulous if Nick doesn't work out."

"I think Nick will work out just fine."

Meghan smiled as she closed the door. She couldn't wait to do the Cinderella thing. She was half scared and half excited, but totally committed. Tonight would be the beginning of something wonderful. She took a small green paisley book from her tote bag and went out on the balcony.

The man she dreamed about now had a face and a name. She leaned her head back against the chair, let her eyelids drift shut and let the fantasy sweep her away. Moments later, she opened her eyes, grabbed her pen, and flipped to the first page of her new diary.

The words flew across the paper as she tried to capture the image in her mind. *Nick's green eyes shimmer with an inner fire as he stares at Elise. When he speaks, his one-word command is rough with desire. "Strip," he says and she slowly peels off her dress...*

ALEX GRABBED a cold beer out of the minibar and headed for the balcony. As he passed through the living room he considered putting that champagne into the fridge, but he'd probably never drink the stuff. Then he noticed Meghan's blue journal on the coffee table.

His conscience pricked him over keeping the book of fantasies. He assumed Meghan had been too distracted to remember, but he couldn't forget it. He picked it up and, with perfect recall, imagined the entry he read before, except now the man and woman beneath the waterfall were him and Meghan.

He plundered her sweet mouth and slid her wet, naked body onto his, listening to her cry out in pleasure... He glanced at his watch and decided he had time to read a little more.

A while later, Alex reached for his beer. His mouth had gone dry about six pages ago. The bottle was empty. He wasted a couple of seconds debating whether to get another one. Instead, he lit a cigarette, then turned the page to the next entry. Just one more...

He got caught up in the wildly erotic scenes she'd created. As he read, he couldn't help but compare the journal personality to the real woman. A profile emerged and he figured he had Meghan pegged. Smart, well-educated, middle-class professional. Sexual dynamite primed to blow a hole through the heart of the first man who touched her the right way. He wanted to be that man.

As he crushed out the half-smoked cigarette, he couldn't dismiss the possibility that it was all an act. The journal, the seductive innocence, the blushing attempts to flirt. Everything could have been carefully calculated to get past his defenses. After that mess in Overtown, Braga would be wary of another double-cross.

Alex closed the journal as the evening shadows stretched farther across the balcony, tilting his head to ease the kink in his neck. He also needed to ease the bulge in his jeans before meeting Meghan for dinner.

After a quick but satisfying shower, he shaved and got dressed. He slipped the journal into the breast pocket of his sports jacket on his way out the door, wondering whether to return it before or after they ate. He stepped off the elevator and walked across the lobby to the small lounge just off the atrium. He scanned the cocktail-hour crowd until he spotted Meghan at a corner table.

Whoa.

She wore a pale-pink dress that flowed over her body like water. He could see that the open buttons at the neckline revealed the swell of her breasts. The short skirt rode up her thighs, showing off the length of caramel skin. Her shapely calves crossed at the ankles and her feet were bare. Another pair of "seduce me" sandals lay abandoned under the table.

Alex forced his gaze to her face. She wasn't wearing her glasses. She'd done something to make those gorgeous brown eyes appear smoky, mysterious. Her lips were painted a slick, glossy pink. Just looking at her was getting him hard again.

What was she wearing under that dress? The black lace bikini set? No, it would show through the pink fabric. The white satin one was more likely. Smiling as he moved toward her, he could just imagine the smooth material covering her sexy—

Alex stopped abruptly.

He was so focused on Meghan he didn't see the man sitting with her—a man he knew very well. Memories assaulted him and he closed his eyes briefly. Gunshots. Chaos. The smell of blood. Blinding pain. The scar on his temple started throbbing and a wave of nausea swept over him.

He slid behind a marble pillar, waiting for the anxiety to pass but keeping Meghan in sight. He studied Rogelio Braga's salt-and-pepper hair, impeccable tailoring, old world manners. If he wasn't a drug trafficking felon, Alex might even have liked him.

He touched his fingers to the book in his jacket. To think *he'd* been sorry about deceiving *her*.

His gut twisted again. His hope that she wasn't connected with the cartel vanished as he watched her laugh at something Braga said. Were they discussing him, and how she'd played him? Braga had invited "Nicholas" to Cayo Sueño in appreciation of him saving the man's life. Ms. Foster, if that was really her name, must be the reward after all. Shit!

He wanted to believe Meghan wasn't part of this, that the room mix-up was pure coincidence. But, thinking about the woman in her journal, he acknowledged that she was doing one hell of a job hiding her true personality. He must be losing his edge to have been taken in so easily.

Alex watched Braga place his hand on her forearm as he spoke. When Meghan nodded, he got up and walked away. She sat quietly for a moment before looking around the cocktail lounge. Her eyes moved in his direction and Alex stepped out from behind the pillar.

She waved eagerly when she spotted him. If she were for real, he'd have cherished the greeting. Instead, he was pissed off that he'd fallen for the act, fallen for her. He scrutinized her as he strode toward the table. There was nothing but genuine pleasure in her smile, no pretence or deceit.

Lord, let him be wrong.

"Hi, Nick!" She indicated the chair beside hers. "I was beginning to wonder if you stood me up."

Nick. Yeah, that's right. We both have roles to play, don't we? He lowered himself into the seat, keeping his gaze fixed on her face. "You didn't look lonely."

"What? Oh. That was just small talk. I wasn't planning to throw you over for him." She gave him a teasing smile and her hands fluttered to her lap. She seemed giddy, nervous. Guilty?

"Who was he?" Even as he said it, the flat inflection of his tone revealed more than he intended.

Meghan blinked in surprise. "Nobody. He just recognized me from the welcome reception."

He studied her carefully, but didn't see any of the physical signs he'd been trained to look for. Then again, his instincts about women had failed him before. "You seemed to be pretty deep in conversation."

"You seem to notice a lot for someone who just showed up."

He acknowledged her quick retort with a slight grin. As far as he could figure, she was neither lying nor being evasive. For the moment. "Sorry. Army recon habits die hard."

The frown lines cleared from her brow, as did the tension in her shoulders. She leaned to one side of her chair, her elbow resting on the arm. The shift caused her dress to gap slightly, giving him a nice view of the lace edges of her pink bra.

He didn't remember her having this much cleavage. She must be wearing one of those lift-up push-together things. Not that he minded. She looked great. He just wanted to know why.

"So what were you two talking about?"

"He was telling me about the ruins on the east side of the island. Apparently, he's a regular guest here at the resort."

"He was just following Julie's advice, huh? Making sure you have a good time? I thought that was my job."

His gaze followed the fingers of one hand as she traced circles over the opposite wrist. Her gestures had a different energy tonight. Either her innate sensuality had been unleashed or the move was well rehearsed. Against his better judgment, he was seriously turned on. Meghan wasn't the only one who wanted to explore some erotic fantasies.

"You haven't been hired yet." She angled her head and regarded him from across the table. Her hot-pink lips tilted in a haughty smirk. "First of all, there's a dress code."

"Hey, this is one of my favorite shirts." He held open one side of his sports jacket to give her a better view of the green-and-orange pattern.

"I'd hate to see what you passed over. All you need is a parrot and a rapier to complete the look."

More fantasies. More games. Fine. He was willing if it got his badge restored. He lowered his voice to an intimate level. "If you don't like it, I'll take it off. We can play the Lusty Pirate and the Tavern Wench."

"That sounds like an interesting fantasy."

"It's one of many. I'll tell you some other ones later."

With a delighted grin, she leaned back in her chair. "Okay, the job is yours. How much do you charge?"

"I work on the barter system. Why don't we start the negotiations over dinner?" He stood and went around to her chair.

"I should warn you, I intend to drive a *hard* bargain."

He chuckled. "Let the games begin."

Alex extended his hand to help her up, glad for the chance to touch her. Holding Meghan's soft fingers while she slipped her sandals back on, he was again treated to a glimpse of her cleavage. When she stood, their eyes met briefly and he knew she'd flashed him on purpose.

More than her looks had been revamped. Whatever the cause, he really liked her new confidence. A bold sensuality hummed just below the surface. The new Meghan was a woman sure of herself and her appeal.

Alex matched his gait to hers as they walked across the lobby toward Breezes, the outdoor restaurant. He admired the view as she strode ahead of him, head high and shoulders back. That sexy little swing to her hips sent a shudder of longing through him.

Meghan glanced over one shoulder, her whiskey-colored eyes twinkling as if she wanted to make sure he was watching. Alex couldn't have looked away if he tried. And, by the smug little grin on her pretty mouth, she knew it.

Yeah. He definitely liked the change. Trouble was dangerously fascinating.

But at the same time, her transition was so swift and so complete, he had to question it. Besides, the last thing he needed was to get involved with a possible suspect. Internal Affairs would just love that.

He swept his gaze around the restaurant, cataloguing faces as he scanned the diners. He saw Rogelio Braga approach the bar across the veranda with two other men. One he recognized as a known trafficker from the hot sheets at the Miami office, but he didn't know the third.

He looked back at Meghan.

Maybe he'd jumped to conclusions. Her conversation with Braga could have been as innocent as she'd made out. Then again, maybe it wasn't. Either way, Alex intended to hold on to her journal for a while longer. It was the best way to find out who she really was.

He'd also ask his partner to do a background check. He had to know if she was involved with the Miami cartel. But he couldn't lie to himself. Something about her touched him on a level he'd almost forgotten existed. His interest was personal.

4

My whole body, my whole being, is on fire for his touch. I am overcome by need, ripe with longing for a man I've never met before and don't intend to see again.

"GOOD EVENING, Miss Meghan. Good evening, sir."

The maitre d' of Breezes welcomed them as they approached the entrance. He led them toward an intimate table overlooking the Gulf. "Enjoy your meal."

She started to sit, but Nick took her arm. Her skin tingled at his touch and she turned her head to look up at him. He seemed distracted and an odd expression crossed his face, one she couldn't interpret.

"Is something wrong?"

He smiled, but his gaze still focused over her shoulder as he maneuvered her to the opposite chair. "You'll have a better view of the water from here."

She still didn't have his full attention. How was she supposed to seduce him if he wouldn't look at her? When he took his seat, she tried another "Elise move." She leaned back in her chair, resting her left elbow on the arm. Her fingers skimmed across her collarbone, back and forth.

She had all of his attention now. The look in his light green eyes could only be described as penetrating, his expression a heady blend of fascination and desire. Knowing that Nick wanted her sent a jolt of excitement through her. She felt powerful, feminine, wildly erotic.

She watched Nick watching her. His gaze slowly roamed her body, pausing on her breasts. She wondered if he was undressing her with his eyes. Arousal warmed her skin and sent pulses of desire throughout her body. She met his grin with a confident smile of her own.

If he were to undress her now, he'd discover her delicious secret. She shifted on her chair, uncrossing her ankles to enjoy the slide of one bare leg against the other. The change of position made her intensely aware of her new thong panties.

With a quiet intake of breath, she imagined Nick's fingertips delving under the satin edge, stroking her damp flesh… Heat rushed to her cheeks as she took a sip of her water, hoping to cool off.

"You're staring at me, Nick."

"Yeah. I am."

Grinning in smug delight, she basked in the discovery of her new appeal. Maybe clothes did make the woman. She'd traded her glasses for contact lenses and styled her hair into soft ringlets. Julie's skillfully applied cosmetics emphasized her eyes and transformed her lips into a sultry pout. Meghan almost hadn't recognized herself in the mirror.

The dress she'd borrowed had looked so sweet and breezy hanging in the closet. Its pale-pink color and flared skirt seemed too innocent for seduction. Julie had smirked, then convinced her to try it on.

Ooh, baby.

"Do you like what you see?"

"You know I do, Trouble."

The waiter came back to take their orders. Nick asked for a manly portion of red meat and potatoes while she chose the prawns in beurre blanc with wild mushroom risotto. She couldn't help but giggle over their choice of entrees. Opposites did attract. The pivotal question was, would they wrinkle the sheets anytime soon?

Nick rested his elbows on the table and laced his fingers. He tilted his head, regarding her with an attentive expression and a raised eyebrow. "So tell me more about yourself."

"What would you like to know?"

"Everything."

She narrowed her eyes and leaned back, dropping her hands to her lap. The whole point of acting out her fantasies was to keep things impersonal. If they knew too much about each other, it might cause complications at the end of the week.

"Where's the fun in knowing everything? There won't be any secrets or surprises left to discover."

A shadow crossed his features, darkened his eyes. "Guess I'll have to settle for whatever you reveal."

"I'm five-feet eight-inches tall. I refuse to tell you my weight." She batted her lashes.

"Fascinating." His tone of voice belied the word. "I'm more interested in whether you're seeing anyone, if you have plans for tomorrow and whether you sleep in the nude."

She smiled at the waiter who brought her salad before turning her attention back to Nick. "Not involved. No plans. Not telling."

"You're on vacation. Why not try something different, something you've never done before?" His voice was rich with challenge, low and sexy.

Meghan drew in a quick breath. Was she that obvious? If so, seducing Nick would be easier than she'd thought. "I'd love to be adventurous. Do you have any ideas?"

"How about joining me for a tour of the Dry Tortugas? The national park is supposed to have great snorkeling."

Snorkeling? Unless it was a new euphemism for sex, that wasn't exactly what she had in mind. "Um, sure. That sounds fun."

"Is there something else you want to do instead?"

She hesitated. Did she dare mention it? Elise would. "My sister told me there's a nude beach on the southwest shore."

"I prefer to show my body to only one woman at a time, thanks. I sleep naked, though, in case you wondered."

What a visual. Nick's long, lean body stretched across a white sheet wearing only a fine gloss of sweat…

"I'll keep that in mind." She tried to match his casual tone but the catch in her voice betrayed her interest. Had it been this hot a minute ago? She took another sip of her wine.

"On the other hand, you don't strike me as the *au naturel* type. I'll bet you sleep in one of those lace things I saw in your luggage."

"That's for me to know and you to find out."

Meghan shot him a coy glance from under her lashes and wriggled her brows.

He flashed her the friendly-sexy grin. "Want to play the Fashion Model and the Photographer?"

She laughed, her fork paused in midair. "What's with you and the theme games?"

"A guy can dream."

"Dream on, Nick." She lowered her voice, made her tone alluring, and changed a phrase that was normally a rebuff into an invitation.

It seemed she'd found a guy who liked fantasies almost as much as she. Could he be any more perfect? Nick was definitely her Mr. Fabulous. All she had to do was find the right time to mention her plan.

"You have salad dressing on your mouth, Meghan. Want me to get it for you?"

"No, but thanks for offering."

Heat flared in his eyes and he shifted around in his seat as he watched her lick the drop of Creamy Italian from her lip. She really wanted to be licking *his* lips. And neck and chest and stomach and... And if she didn't stop picturing him naked she was going to explode right here and now.

"Okay, Trouble. Quit holding out on me and get personal."

She wanted to get personal all right. But not about her snuggly flannel pajamas. "I usually just sleep in my panties."

"Which panties? The tiny little blue ones with—?"

"Start talking, Nick. I'm not going to be the only one playing True Confessions. Where's the most unusual place you ever had sex? Do you self-indulge in bed or the shower? How do you like to—?"

"Hold it." He looked a little shocked. Obviously he hadn't expected her to be so blunt. "Let's change the subject."

"Chicken."

"Fine. I once had sex in a stalled elevator for two hours."

Her pulse quickened and she reminded herself to breathe. One of the entries in her diary involved an elevator, a strange man and a melting pint of ice cream. "You were stuck for two hours or had sex for two hours?"

"Sex for two hours. Impressed?"

"That depends. Are you bragging or flirting?"

He turned his smile up a notch, a cocky expression on his handsome face. His smoke-roughened voice dropped to a purr of sound. "There're two things I do well, darlin'. And flirting is the other one."

Omigod. Now it was really hot. Well, she could flirt too. She slipped off her right sandal and crossed her legs at the knee. She wiggled her foot until it came in contact with his ankle. Nick shifted as though it had been an accident, so she did it again, this time rubbing her toes along his shin.

His beautiful green eyes issued an invitation from their smoldering depths. Her heart fluttered and a sweet tingling pressure bubbled in her belly.

"Seems like there's a storm brewing."

She looked at him questioningly.

"It might be the right time for that rain check."

She grinned at his reference to the rain check for seeing her in the red lace panties, then lied through her teeth. "I'm not the least bit wet..."

"Watch out. Some men would take that as a challenge."

"Some men might not be *up* to the challenge."

"I consider myself a man who's *outstanding* in that regard."

Meghan rested her chin on clasped hands, looking him over slowly. "That's a very healthy ego you've got, Nick."

"I also have very healthy…appetites."

The sensual hunger his voice conveyed sent a rush of need straight between her thighs. All of her senses were aroused, making her hyperaware of the gorgeous male sitting across from her. *Ask him. Just come right out and ask him.*

A dark form caught her attention and she turned to see the maitre d'. He apologized for the intrusion before leaning down to murmur in Nick's ear.

"Now?" His brows drew together and the corners of his mouth turned down. He cursed under his breath in annoyance. "Thank you."

"What's the matter?" She stared in amazement and her sexual anticipation evaporated like mist. The charming man she'd been talking to had vanished before her eyes. A stranger with tight features and a hard voice sat in his place.

"Nick?"

He looked up as if she'd startled him. He glanced over her shoulder, still frowning, then his expression cleared. "I'm sorry, Meghan. There's some business I've got to take care of."

"You're supposed to be on vacation, too."

"A working vacation, remember? I'm here at the

request of an important client. Since he's footing the bill, I can't ignore him—as much as I'd like to.''

"Do you have to leave right now? You haven't eaten yet." It was a lame attempt to keep him there and they both knew it.

He pasted on a smile but the expression didn't reach his eyes. "Sorry. This can't wait. I'll see you later, I promise."

Hugging her arms about her waist, Meghan watched him walk away. Her fantasy deserted her with every step he took. This was hardly the way she'd imagined the night would end. She glanced around the restaurant. Everyone was probably snickering at the pitiful woman who'd been dumped by her date.

So much for being a Sex Goddess in Training.

ALEX SLAMMED THE DOOR of his suite behind FBI Special Agent Emelio Sanchez, his partner since being assigned to the Special Operations Division and his best friend since college.

Emelio tossed a handful of cashews into his mouth as he walked into the living room. "You're pissed because I interrupted some dinner date? Meantime, I had to raid the minibar for a meal." He rolled his eyes as he sank into an armchair and planted his heels on the coffee table.

Yeah, he was pissed. Alex couldn't remember the last time he'd been so completely fascinated by a woman. "This had better be good."

"It is good, man. I just got word that Frankie Ramos's yacht, the *Cielo Blanco,* is docked over on Key West."

Alex stopped pacing and bared his teeth in a feral grin. "So, Braga's boss finally surfaced. Excellent."

"Well, the boat's here. He's not on it."

"What? Where is he?"

Emelio scowled and ducked his head. "We're not sure yet."

The image of Meghan's face filled his mind, followed by an image of that body in that dress. "Great, partner. My dinner's cold and my date is probably colder. You dragged me up here for—"

"I dragged you up here because Easton wants you to call him. Pronto, if not sooner, and I'm quoting." Brent Easton was their direct supervisor at the SOD. He was also a demanding son of a bitch.

"Shit. That can't possibly be good." Alex dropped onto the couch and massaged the still tender scar on his temple. "We better find out where Ramos has gone to ground."

"It's only a matter of time. We'll get him."

"That's what you said six weeks ago," Alex grumbled.

His partner's voice was deceptively calm when he made an anatomically impossible suggestion.

"Sorry, Em. That was a lousy thing to say." Alex dragged both hands through his hair, sighing heavily.

"Forget it." Emelio crumpled the empty nut bag in his fist and arced it into the trashcan.

"This case should have been one for the books. Instead we're scrambling to recover ground." Alex had taken the lead after his friend got too close to a witness, an informant he'd felt sorry for. Gina had been a young woman caught in an impossible situation. She'd had no real choice but to betray him. Now, Braga, and who knew how many others could make Emelio for a cop.

"Let's not rehash old business, partner."

Emelio was right, but that incident had been a turning point in Alex's career. Problem was, he didn't know which way it had pushed him. *Concentrate on the here and now,* he told himself. "Okay. What have you heard?"

"Word on the street says Ramos is really losing it." Emelio grabbed two beers out of the minibar and passed one over. "Spends more time supporting his habit than taking care of business. Some of the laundered money might even be in his private accounts instead of the cartel's."

Alex whistled in mock admiration. "Frankie must have balls of cold-rolled steel. Drug czars aren't exactly known for their benevolence."

"That or the shit he's putting up his nose has fried his brain cells. Let's focus on him. If we can break Ramos, he'll flip on the rest in exchange for a light sentence."

Alex rolled the beer bottle between his palms. "Rogelio Braga needs to be watched. I don't think it's a coincidence he invited me here this particular week."

Em shook his head. "Forget Braga for now. If we get Ramos, we break the Miami cartel. Cocaine addiction makes a man paranoid and unpredictable, but it also makes him vulnerable."

"Something big is going down. Braga had dinner with some heavy hitters tonight." Alex stared at the ceiling, speaking slowly, running scenarios in his head. "He's gathering his strength for a change of leadership.

That's going to fall out on participants, bystanders and innocents alike.''

"You've never been innocent, man.'' Emelio scoffed, trying to make a joke of his concern.

But Alex hoped that Meghan was. He pulled the slim blue journal from his jacket. "Listen. I need you to run a check on somebody. Name's Meghan Elise Foster. Her luggage is from Baltimore. Find out for me if she's legit.''

"I take it she was your date.'' Emelio studied his face, seeing more than Alex wanted him to, as usual. "You think the lady is a player?''

"Could be. She was cozy with Braga earlier tonight. Then she came on to me. There's another factor that points to her innocence, but I need to be sure.''

His partner nodded. "I'll put her name through the usual databases and see if I come up with anything. In the meantime, order me some food, will you? I'm starving.''

Alex called room service and ordered for both of them. It didn't look like he'd get back to Meghan after all. Next he dialed from memory a number in Miami. The first call would automatically transfer to another line in case anyone checked the resort's telephone log. While the phone rang, he lay back on the couch and adjusted the pillow behind his head.

"Hello? This is Brent Easton.''

Alex didn't waste time on pleasantries. "It's me. Em is with me. We're checking in.''

Easton's voice boomed over the telephone line. "Where the hell have you two been? I paged him an hour ago!''

"We're making progress.''

"You'd better be. I'm getting flak from above and, trust me, I intend to send it down your way."

Didn't he always? Alex held onto his patience with effort. "Braga contacted me, though we haven't hooked up. Em has solid information that Ramos is on his way here, if he's not here already."

"It's a decent start but you have to move on this. You've got the rest of the week to get squared away. After that, the Ramos case is turned over to someone else."

"The hell it is!" Alex sat up so quickly the pillow fell to the floor. He struggled to hold onto his temper, which had been dangerously short of late. "We've been building the case against Ramos for two years, Brent. You're not taking us off it. Not when we're so close—"

"You'd better play this one by the book, Alex. Do you hear me? Any action you take will be called into question until Internal Affairs clears you on the shooting."

He scowled. Like he needed the reminder. Both he and Emelio had been on admin probation until this latest break in the case. "IAD can kiss my ass. I did what I had to to get the job done."

"You know, you've got a real attitude problem lately."

"Yeah, well, you can tell me all about it when you quit riding a desk. I haven't lost my edge," he said it as much to convince himself as his boss.

"Hell, if anything, your edges are too jagged," Brent muttered. "Bring me up to speed."

"'Nick Alexander' is definitely going to be brought into play. Since Manny Ortega got busted, Ramos needs another underground banker for the Miami operation. I'll use Braga to get to him and get the info we need."

"The Attorney General is demanding enough evidence to present to a federal grand jury. She wants it yesterday. Don't screw up on this one."

The line went dead before Alex could say another word. He hung up the phone, then looked around for his cigarettes. He felt the past stalking him like a dark shadow. Maybe he *had* lost his edge, those sharp instincts that too often meant the difference between making or breaking a case. Overtown had been a major screw-up. His.

He should have seen it coming. Somehow, he should have seen it. Emelio got too close to their informant but Alex backed him up in front of the brass, despite his misgivings. As a result, two people died and the bad guys got in the wind.

The underlying guilt made him think about Greg. Not long after he joined the DEA, his younger brother overdosed. All Greg's life, Alex did his best to protect him. It was a hard truth to face that his best hadn't been good enough.

Had it ever been enough? How long was it since he felt like he made any kind of difference? For eight years, he'd waded through the cesspool of the drug underworld. He'd kept friends and family at a distance in order to immerse himself in The Life. And still his sacrifices came down to bureaucratic bullshit and overturned convictions.

He was really starting to hate this damned job.

Wandering over to the French doors, he stepped out onto the balcony. He tapped the cigarette pack until one slid out, then pinched off the end. The stress he'd been under lately made it hard to quit. Smoking half a cigarette didn't seem as bad.

He felt as if he was moving through life instead of living it. There was an emptiness inside him and he wasn't sure who the hell he was anymore. Two months ago he was Andy Ruiz. Today he was Nick Alexander. And next week? Next month?

Emelio came out to stand beside him, resting his elbows on the railing. "I take it the brass is stepping up the pressure?"

He sucked in nicotine and stared into the distance. "I learned something when I was under deep cover in the Southwest a few years back, hombre."

Emelio turned his head to look at him.

"I roughed up informants, watched criminals kill each other without losing any sleep. I even went so far as sampling the product to secure my identity. If you can name it, I probably did it."

"I know, man. Your rep preceded you. What's your point?"

"Supervisors usually look the other way when you cross the line, just as long as you get results and make them look good. Not this time. This time it's all on the line."

"Closing the Ramos case will go a long way to restoring our badges." Emelio gave him a smile that didn't reach his eyes. "But maybe we should look into that investigation firm we've talked about."

Alex shook his head and blew a stream of smoke into the night air. "We've got a mission and nothing's going to keep me from seeing it through. This job means everything to me, Em. It's all I've got."

5

The night is dark and restless and so am I as I wait for my green-eyed lover—

No. Start again.

Moonlight glitters on his dark hair as I stand naked before him, eager for the dangerous pleasure of his touch—

MEGHAN CLOSED HER DIARY and set it beside her on the sofa. She'd been trying to create a new entry, but couldn't seem to concentrate. An odd sense of loss settled heavily in her chest as she stared out at the darkness.

Her resolve had been badly shaken by Nick's sudden exit. It was as if her fantasy man—and her confidence—had walked out with him. Feeling totally rejected, she planned to stay here in her suite and sulk. Maybe order something chocolate from room service.

She'd felt something for Nick, a kind of tenuous emotional connection, as well as the physical attraction. The electric spark of awareness whenever they touched was her main reason for choosing him. Was she wrong in thinking he felt it, too?

Probably. Heaven knew she'd been wrong before. Frowning, she stood up and went to open the window. The lights around the Cascade Pool caught her attention. She'd forgotten about the party Julie invited her to.

Okay. No more sulking. She wasn't going to follow the same old path, just because it was safe and familiar. She was going to find a vacation lover and have some fun before going back to school. Grabbing her card key, she headed for the door.

"Welcome to the Singles Mingle," read the banner that hung over the walkway leading to the pool. A cool breeze ruffled her hair while she hesitated on the edge of the stone patio. Taking a deep breath, she tried to ignore her anxiety. She could do this. She'd found one great guy. She could find another.

Still she hesitated. People wandered among intimate groups or danced on the white sand. Everyone was trying, desperately in her opinion, to impress everyone else. Just then one rowdy bunch of men called out, "Hey, Julie's sister, over here!"

The enthusiastic greeting sent her straight toward the bar. She needed a little more courage before she went on the manhunt. One of the bartenders grinned as she elbowed her way onto a padded stool. His name tag read "Alfonso."

He raised his voice so she could hear him above the Salsa music. "Hi, Julie's sister."

She smiled and leaned forward against the bar. "Not you, too. Call me Meghan."

"How about something cold, Meghan? We Jamaicans know what to do with fresh fruit and lotsa ice."

"Thank you." She twisted sideways on the stool and

scanned the crowd. Maybe Nick would show up. Maybe he'd finish with his client early and come find her.

Julie suddenly appeared at her shoulder. "Hi, Megs! I didn't think you were going to come. Where's your pirate?"

"Feeding his parrot, I guess." She dropped her gaze and frowned, drumming her fingertips on the top of the bar.

"It didn't work out with him, huh? Well, in that case, why are you sitting here instead of circulating? You're not going to find Mr. Fabulous this way."

"Take a breath, Jules. I'll go mingle as soon as Alfonso finishes making my drink."

Her sister looked startled by the glass of multicolored slush he placed in front of her. "You made her a Miami Vice?"

Alfonso shrugged and gave her a grin. "You told me to push tonight's drink special."

Meghan eyed the glass suspiciously. She didn't drink as a rule, but she needed to relax. Cautiously, she took a sip and wrinkled her nose. Rum, with strawberry and piña colada. She wasn't sure about the blue stuff floating on top and decided not to ask.

"Come on, Megs, bring it with you. I'm going to introduce you to some of the Fabulous candidates I've picked."

"How did you know Nick wouldn't work out?"

"I didn't." Jules grinned. "I picked these guys for me. Let's go and find you a boy toy!"

She cocked her head toward Alfonso, who was blatantly eavesdropping. "Why don't you just announce my intentions over the loudspeaker?"

"Hey, I could be a boy toy," he offered.

Julie glanced over her shoulder. "Forget it, Casanova. You know the rule about messing with the guests."

Alfonso winked at Meghan and stuck his tongue out at Julie before greeting another customer.

"I did my best to weed out the losers, but there was only so much I could ask and still be subtle."

"You're renowned for your subtlety, Jules. Like at the welcome reception this afternoon."

She took another sip of her cocktail while her sister yammered on about all of the eligible bachelors at the party. She liked the way the rum made her feel. Edgy and warm and a little daring.

The same way she felt around Nick.

Well, forget him. She'd settle for—*choose* someone else. There were plenty of good-looking men here tonight. They might look silly to an outsider trying to remain aloof, but the people she earlier labeled as desperate were having fun.

"I can be fun," she muttered aloud.

"Of course you can, sweetie. You're lots of fun. First, I want you to meet Bobby." Julie introduced her to the Australian diving instructor and then faded into the crowd.

"Hallo, swee'hart. You're a right beauty."

Bobby gave her the old once-over and widened his smile. Her confidence started to rise. He had a muscular build, golden hair and a nice smile. *Okay, Megs. Be fun. Be sexy.* She tried to picture Bobby in one of her fantasies, but just couldn't pull it off.

The Australian was tall and handsome, intelligent and virile. Too virile. After only a few minutes, she noticed he never maintained eye contact. Not with her, anyway. Bobby's gaze wandered to any female that got within twenty feet of him.

"Hi. Remember me?" She snapped her fingers in front of his face to get his attention. "I'm leaving."

When she made her way back to the bar to return her empty glass, Alfonso smiled encouragingly. He'd obviously decided to join in the matchmaking fun, but she drew the line when he tried to introduce her to a couple of university students.

"I appreciate your help, Alfonso. Really, I do. But would you stop giving my name to college boys? A kegger is hardly my idea of a romantic evening." She lifted her empty glass and pointed her index finger. "Quit laughing and make me another one of these things."

"Don't worry about it, Meghan. Things can only get better from here."

Keeping that philosophy in mind, she agreed to dance with Frank, a graphics designer from Los Angeles.

He wasn't Nick but he had possibilities. He was tall and handsome, successful and worldly. Too worldly. Frank eventually revealed that he liked for two girls to spank him with dry spaghetti noodles.

"I prefer my noodles cooked, thanks." She excused herself and went looking for Julie.

"I thought you said you weeded out the losers?" she complained when she found her. "I'm not into pasta sex."

"So I made a mistake." Her sister shrugged. "That doesn't mean you can give up. There are lots of great guys here and I want you to meet them all. You're supposed to mingle at a singles party.''

The great guy she wanted to be with was nowhere in sight so she was wasting her time. She sighed. Then again, she had nothing better to do. Determined to keep looking, she accepted another glass of multicolored slush from Alfonso. *Meghan Foster, party animal. Grrr.* She giggled and wondered how much vice was in these little drinks.

''Okay. Who's next?'' Meghan demanded.

Her sister hustled her over to a group of salesmen. After that Julie left her with a college professor, followed by a trio of Japanese computer software developers. She couldn't picture any of them in her fantasies either.

Evan, an art gallery owner from New York, was her next dance partner. He was tall and handsome, cultured and sensitive. Too sensitive. Didn't it just figure? Evan was gay. He'd only come to the party to make his boyfriend jealous. When the music ended, so did Meghan's tolerance.

Julie found her sitting alone by the bar. ''What's wrong? Why aren't you mingling?''

She moved closer to be heard over the music. ''I quit. Your grand scheme isn't working.''

''So my first choices haven't panned out.'' Julie crossed her arms and frowned. ''You have to keep looking if you're going to find the right man. Let me introduce you to a few more—''

She dug in her heels when Julie tried to pull her toward yet another group of men on the make. ''Enough. I mean it.''

Her sister grudgingly left her alone and went back

to the party. Meghan drew patterns in the condensation on her glass, trying to decide how much longer she would stay. She'd already found the right man. Her body hadn't reacted to anyone the way it did around Nick.

The way it was reacting now…

"I took my shirt off for you."

The instant he murmured in her ear, she recognized Nick's gruff voice and freshly showered scent. Her heart gave a little leap as she twisted on the bar stool. Lord, he was gorgeous.

Lust gave her a heightened sense of awareness of the angles and planes of his face, from the light gleaming on his dark hair to the laugh lines bracketing his eyes and finally his utterly kissable mouth.

Glad for the excuse to touch him, Meghan reached out to feel his shirt. The red-and-purple material was silky between her fingers, but it was still revolting. "This isn't much of an improvement. I doubt Don Ho put up much of a fight when you stole his wardrobe."

Nick smirked at her joke then flagged Alfonso for a beer. He stood so close she could feel the heat emanating from his body. Or maybe it was her own body heat making her thighs tingle.

"I didn't think I'd see you again tonight," she said.

"We didn't finish getting personal."

The underlying sensuality of his words and the silky rasp of his voice played havoc with her. Her breasts felt heavy and a throbbing ache pulsed in her belly. She dipped her chin, glancing coyly from under her lashes. "I'm all for getting personal."

"Glad to hear it, Trouble." He arched one brow at her before taking a sip of his beer, then setting the bottle on the bar. "So. Our friend here tells me that you're looking for a stud-muffin."

She whipped her head around and caught Alfonso grinning at them. "Stop matchmaking and start drink-making. You're almost as bad as Julie."

The young bartender hastily went to take an order farther down the bar.

"He thought maybe I'd be a good candidate." Nick paused, a gleam of humor lighting his eyes. "Of course, I told him you're not really my type."

Brows furrowed in mock insult, Meghan set her glass on the bar with a snap. "What is that supposed to mean? You didn't seem to mind my type earlier."

"Oh, there's not too much wrong with you—"

"Thanks a lot."

"I like my women a little on the trashy side." He held up a hand to stop her reaction. "Sorry, it's a song title—I'm a country music fan."

She rolled her eyes dramatically. "Heaven help me. Ugly shirts and country music, too?"

"All I meant was that I normally go for scarlet-lipped, line-dancing, beer-drinking gals. Until you, that is."

She appreciated the compliment. But she was trying to *ruin* her reputation. "I drank a beer once."

"You're a wild one, all right." Nick teased. "It would take a lot of beer for you to have any less class."

"Do you think trashy women are more fun?"

The amusement faded from his eyes and his expression was inscrutable. "They're uncomplicated. The last thing you are."

"I'm not complicated. My needs are really quite simple." She rested her chin on her palm. "But every guy that Julie introduced tonight was a loser in some way.''

''I guess I still have a chance then.''

''Oh, you're definitely in the running. As long as you're not a gigolo, a pervert, a homosexual or a cop.''

Physically, Nick didn't move a rock-hard muscle. Yet he still managed to give the impression that he'd retreated several feet. ''That sure makes your opinion clear.''

Meghan mentally smacked a palm against her forehead. Why did she have to bring *that* up? She'd been thinking about the Mr. Fabulous contestants, but the last part slipped out before she realized what she'd said. Those Miami Vice drinks had obviously loosened her tongue. Way to go, Megs.

She made a sweeping motion with her hand, as if she could erase her words. ''I didn't mean to say that cops are all bad.''

''But you did. So, what's your problem with cops?'' His eyes contained shadows that created a kaleidoscope of shifting emotion. He drained a full third of his beer in one swallow.

''My brother-in-law was a police officer.''

''Was?''

Stupid! The seductive mood was broken and she had only herself to blame. Meghan tightened her grip on the glass as he waited for her to elaborate. After another mouthful of frozen slush, she answered his earlier question instead.

''I don't have a problem with cops. Just getting too close to them. There were too many nights I stayed with Jules when Kyle didn't come home. She was always anxious and scared until she heard that key turn in the door.''

Nick pulled a cigarette out of his pocket and pinched off the end before lighting it. ''So he quit the force?''

She had no intention of discussing the shooting, or her own culpability. ''Why did you break your cigarette in half?''

He studied her as he inhaled, as if deciding whether or not to pursue the topic. Then he carefully blew the smoke away from her. ''I've been trying to quit.''

She slowly exhaled as well, grateful he let the other subject drop. ''It's a terrible habit, very unhealthy.''

''Yeah, I know. I started back when I was in the Army. Not much else to do on field maneuvers.'' He signaled Alfonso for another beer before looking back at her. ''So, what criteria are you using for the stud-muffin position anyway?''

His leg brushed against hers as he changed his stance. The brief touch of soft denim on her bare leg scrambled her senses. Or maybe it was the Miami Vice going to her head.

''Um, what was— Oh, I remember.'' She ticked off on her fingers. ''I'm supposed to be looking for a guy who is sexy, virile, cultured, successful, worldly, romantic and sensitive.''

''Notice any contradictions here? How is a guy supposed to be virile *and* sensitive?''

Her lips quivered as she acknowledged the ridiculousness of the list she and Julie made. ''It's possible.''

''Only in Mel Gibson movies.'' He chuckled as he glanced around the Singles Mingle. ''Your sister seems to be looking for replacements.''

Meghan reached for her glass and sipped from it, not

bothering to hide her disdain. "Remind me to act enthusiastic when she finds the next loser."

"You wouldn't have to pretend with me." He offered her a sensual, inviting smile.

Was the excitement singing through her veins due to alcohol or to hormones? Nick's eyes held both secrets and promises and his expression was one of heated challenge. No doubt any orgasm with him would be as real as it got. Hormones, definitely hormones.

"Bragging again, Nick?"

"Just the facts, ma'am."

He put one foot up on the brass rail along the bottom of the bar, shifting his weight to the opposite hip. Her gaze dropped to the front of his jeans. Omigod. She stared out at the night sky in order to get her pulse back under control.

"Why is it that whenever I'm near you, Nick, I feel like I'm on a runaway train with no brakes?"

His warm fingers gently brushed her cheek, tilting her chin up until she looked at him. There was an odd tenderness in his face. "Don't worry, I'll keep you safe."

Meghan took a quick breath, delighted by the intensity of his gaze…and that swelling in his jeans. He really did want her. She saw it in his eyes, felt it in his touch.

"Who's going to keep me safe from you?"

"You're looking for trouble and we both know it. But we'll take things slow and easy. That's more my speed."

She took a gulp of her drink and swallowed hard. Fast or slow, she'd take him any way she could get him. "I didn't think you had a speed. I haven't seen you do anything except lounge around and drink beer."

Every move he made was economical and easy, but he had to do something to stay in such great shape. His broad shoulders and muscular chest tapered to a lean torso and flat stomach. She watched the muscles bunch under his skin of his forearm as he caught her fingers and helped her to her feet.

"If you want to see me in action, let's go and dance. It's not a country song, but it's got the same heartbroken sentiment."

He settled her into his arms for the slow, romantic ballad. She'd assumed such a big man would be clumsy or hesitant but he led her confidently around the floor, guiding her into some fancy dips and turns.

Her body fit his perfectly. Or his fit hers perfectly. Whatever. Either way, it felt right to be in his arms, hips swaying and thighs brushing. She'd read somewhere that men who danced well made love even better.

Nick was an excellent dancer.

A current of electric awareness arced between them. Could he possibly be as incredible in bed as he was on the dance floor? She was more than anxious to find out. Meghan sneaked a glance at his profile just as he looked down and winked. He seemed to smile with his whole being, his face alight with pleasure. It was a beautiful sight to behold and impossible not to respond with a smile of her own.

The band played another slow song, so they stayed where they were. She let the soft wail of the saxophone wash over and through her. Nick's hold was confident and somehow intimate as he pressed her against his large body. She melted into his embrace, enjoying the warmth of his arms. Then she tripped over his foot.

Uh-oh. It had to be those Miami Vices.

"Are you okay?" Nick looked down in concern.

She took a moment to analyze her condition. Hot, light-headed, disoriented and turned on. "I think I'm drunk."

"Definitely not my type." He laughed, a rumble of sound that started deep in his chest. He tightened his arms around her to better support her weight. "I like a woman who can hold her liquor."

When the song ended, he guided her back to the bar. "I'm not dancing to any of that disco crap. Hey, Alfonso, can we get some coffee?"

She leaned against his shoulder, angling her head to look up at him. "I don't want coffee. I want another Miami Vice."

"You've had enough 'vice,' I think."

"Nope. I'm the good girl in the family."

He smirked and that was all the encouragement she needed. Tonight, she intended to unleash the Wanton Wench within. If she could stop slurring her words and seeing double.

"It's too bad I'm not your type. I don't like beer, I detest country music and I refuse—*refuse* to get breast implants."

Nick lowered his eyes, his gaze drifting over her body. She instinctively started to withdraw, then stopped. What would Elise do? Let him look. She shifted on the stool, sitting a little straighter to give him a better view.

His tone was intimate and approving when he spoke. "Your breasts are just fine."

*His smooth hands would rub and stroke her sensitive
flesh. He'd cup the weight of them in his palms and
brush the pad of his thumb over her nipples...*

"I'm glad you like them." She nodded her head.
And kept nodding. Anxiety built inside her as she tried
to focus. She poked herself in the nose before remem-
bering she didn't have on her glasses. *Okay. Here goes.
I'm gonna ask him.*

"What's on your mind, Trouble? You've got a dangerous gleam in your eyes."

She was taking an incredible chance, one that might
leave her vulnerable and embarrassed. However,
drunken impulse won over sober caution. She wrapped
her palm over his hand and guided it onto her thigh.

Nick's fingers gripped her leg involuntarily and his
pupils dilated with interest. When he didn't remove his
hand, she took a gulp of breath and blurted out her
proposition.

"I want hot, sweaty, mindless sex. And I want it
with you."

6

I open to the fierce passion of his kiss. His lips are hot, his tongue clever. The kiss exhilarates me, ignites me, sets my soul on fire.

SHE GRINNED as Nick took a sharp breath, then snapped his mouth shut. His expression was both stunned and intrigued.

She was a very bad girl. Meghan slid off the bar stool to stand between his muscular thighs and he caught her about the waist. She liked the way his hands felt. They were strong and steady, while hers seemed to belong to someone else.

She watched her fingers comb through his dark hair. It felt as soft and silky as it looked. She drew her hands over the back of his head and under his jaw. Pressing herself closer to his splayed thighs, she rubbed against the button fly of his jeans.

She wanted him. Now. But a little more enthusiasm on his part would be nice.

"Come on, Nick. Let's get crazy naked."

She felt him shiver as she whispered in his ear. His fingers flexed once then relaxed. When he looked at her, his expression was a mixture of regret and concern. "Why don't I take you up to your room?"

She began shaking her head, but stopped abruptly. It made her dizzy. "No, no, no. That's so predictable." The last thing she wanted was vanilla sex. *Give me Rocky Road, baby. With whipped cream on top.* "I wanna be wild and reckless."

Lust and alcohol coursed through her bloodstream. The alcohol caused her to slur her words. The lust inspired her to grab his hands and guide them around to her rear end.

"Wild and reckless, huh?" He gently stroked his fingers over her hips and sighed loudly. "You're killing me, Trouble."

She swayed before catching herself, placing one palm on his chest for balance. "So, are we gonna boink or what?"

Nick's gaze reflected his indecision, but his tone of voice was resigned. "Meghan, I think maybe we should—"

"No! No thinking. I wanna make love on the sand, with the waves crashing over us, just like in the movies."

She broke away from him and tripped toward the edge of the patio. Thinking of Elise, she threw back her head and smiled, her posture both an invitation and a challenge. With a come-hither look, Meghan crooked her index finger.

"Catch me if you can."

She pulled off her sandals and staggered toward the beach on unsteady legs. The sand beneath her feet felt as cool as the breeze blowing off the water. Checking over one shoulder, she saw Nick was rapidly gaining on her. His long stride more than matched her stumbling gait.

Breathless and laughing, she dropped her shoes when he caught her as she splashed into ankle-deep water. He grasped her shoulders and spun her into his arms. She rested her head against his chest, looking out at the horizon and listening to the beat of his heart. Moonlight danced on the incoming waves like stars scattered on the ocean.

Nick's left hand stroked her back while his right slid up to cradle her neck. The gentle massage made her tremble with desire. Her breasts ached, the nipples tight and throbbing where they made contact with his chest. She nuzzled her cheek against his palm and pressed her body closer to his. Feeling the hard ridge of his erection, need overwhelmed her.

Yes. It was finally going to happen. Her *From Here to Eternity* fantasy was going to come true. Yes, yes, yes.

She tilted her head back to look up at him. His dark hair was disheveled from the wind. The moon cast alternating light and shadows over his face, making his green eyes appear dark as jade and bringing his cheekbones into stark relief. She thought there ought to be a law against a man having such wide, full, sexy lips. *I want him and I'm going to have him.*

"I'm not frigid and I can prove it."

"Never thought you were—"

His voice caught when she rubbed her pelvis against his, the buttons on her dress catching on the placket of his zipper. He groaned when she skimmed her hands over his hips to fondle his tush and then he lowered his head.

She felt his breath mingle with hers and her eyes drifted shut. She waited eagerly for the first touch of his lips. A second passed, a lifetime seemed to follow it. The prolonged anticipation was almost unbearable.

Meghan opened her eyes to find him gazing at her with an unexpected tenderness. His soft fingers lightly grazed her cheek, as if memorizing the contours.

"Um. That feels real nice, Nick, but don't you wanna kiss me?"

"More than you know. Much more than I should."

He cupped her face between his palms. When he brushed his mouth slowly, so slowly, over her lips, she feared she might lose her heart. When his mouth finally covered hers, she feared for her soul.

She closed her eyes again and her knees went weak at the sweet thrill of his touch. His gentle kiss was like a whispered promise. The tip of his tongue traced her upper lip, flicked over the lower, before slipping inside.

She returned the kiss, deepened it, faintly tasting tobacco and cinnamon when she explored his mouth. He angled his head to one side, doing some very interesting things with his tongue. Which did very interesting things to every nerve in her body.

He spread one palm across the small of her back, holding her against him. She moaned, pressing forward to rub one thigh between his legs as her panties grew damp. Her hips began to sway in an age-old rhythm. Hot flames danced through her, making her breasts tingle and her skin itch.

This was better than any fantasy she could write.

The universe seemed to have narrowed to just the

two of them. The world was spinning. Her head was spinning along with it. She felt disoriented and breathless. A warm, inviting fog grew in her mind, beckoning her into the darkness. She drew away and tried to focus on Nick's face, but her vision blurred until everything went black.

MEGHAN SLID out of his arms and collapsed into the shallow surf. He'd been so into that kiss, it took a second before Alex realized what had happened.

He gripped her under the arms, pulling her farther up the beach. Kneeling, he bent over to make sure she was still breathing. Her heartbeat was rapid, but the pulse in her throat felt strong beneath his fingers. He swept the wet tendrils off her brow and brushed some sand from her cheek.

Trouble was out like a light.

Damn. It wasn't like he'd planned to take advantage of her while she was drunk. But he had a healthy ego and a normal libido. Any man would find it difficult to turn down a proposition like hers. If she hadn't passed out, he would have been sorely tempted to fulfill her fantasy of sex on the beach—and a few others.

He reached over to get her shoes before lifting her into his arms. Rising to his feet, he adjusted her dead weight and held her securely against his chest. The heat of her inert body penetrated his shirt through the dampness of her clothes.

He began walking back toward the resort. How the hell was he going to carry an unconscious woman through the lobby? Her sister must have seen them through the border of palms because Julie suddenly appeared at his side.

"Hey! What happened? Is she okay?"

"Too many of those frozen drinks. She'll be fine, but we need to get her back to her room."

Julie lifted Meghan's limp arm, crossed it over her body, and tucked her hand against Alex's side. "I hope she's all right."

He glanced down at Meghan while shifting her weight again. She had yet to move a muscle. "Nothing some sleep and a few aspirins won't cure."

"I really appreciate your help...." She raised her eyebrows questioningly.

"Um, Nick. Nick Alexander."

A grin spread across Julie's face while she eyed him up and down. "So, *you're* the pirate. Hallelujah and pass the breath mints."

"Huh?" His brows drew together in bewilderment.

"Nothing, nothing. I can't leave the party right now. Will you take her upstairs?"

"Sure. Don't worry. I won't let anything happen to her."

"Thanks, Nick. Why don't you take her up that way?" She pointed toward a darkened path. Then she gave him directions to a service elevator so he could avoid unwanted speculation.

Once on the sixth floor, Alex quickly located the door to Meghan's suite. Bending his knees, he dropped her shoes and set her bare feet on the carpet. He hugged her awkwardly, one arm around her waist to keep her upright. Now to find the key.

Her head flopped forward onto his chest when he held her away to look for the pockets of her dress. No visible pockets. Nothing but wet, clingy, translucent pink cotton. He slid his right hand over her hips, trying to feel for a small plastic card. No hidden pockets, either.

Where the hell…? He stopped in midthought and shifted his gaze downward. The only possible place to hide it was in her bra. Alex swallowed hard and took a deep breath. He'd been dying to touch her breasts all night, wondering whether they really would fill his palms. In his imagination, though, she'd at least been awake.

He slipped his fingers beneath the wet fabric, the buttons of her dress grazing his hand as he reached inside. He searched the left cup first, biting back a groan when her nipple beaded at his touch. He found the slim magnetic card key, warm from her body heat, but took his time removing it from her bra.

A bell chimed to indicate the elevator was about to stop on this floor. He quickly slid the card into the lock, and with one foot bracing the door open, he kicked her shoes inside. Then he slid his right arm under her knees, lifted her back into his arms and ducked into the suite.

The layout of the rooms was identical to his, so he headed toward the bedroom. He laid her down before going to get a towel. He dried her hair and face, then rubbed the soft cloth over her arms and legs. Meghan remained lifeless through it all.

Alex tossed the towel onto the night table and started to pull the bedspread over her. He hesitated when he looked at the wet material of her dress. The cotton had plastered itself to her body.

He'd have to take it off. He couldn't leave her like that, in case she caught a chill. Yeah. That was his argument. The truth was he wanted to see what she wore under the sexy little dress.

With one knee on the edge of the bed, he bent down and began to undo the buttons running along the front. He slipped a hand beneath her shoulders and raised her to a sitting position. She flopped onto him while he pulled her arms out of the dress.

After peeling the fabric to her waist, he laid her back on the bed. She had a beautiful body, curves in all the right places. Her smooth golden skin offset the dark pink lace of her bra. His fingers ached to touch her again, to stroke her pliant flesh and feel it heat up under his hands.

Just then, Meghan stirred, moaning softly as she flung out her left arm. She began to roll over in her sleep, allowing him to pull the damp dress away. His brain shut down completely when he saw her underwear.

The hot-pink thong left nothing to the imagination. The top circled her trim waist while the thin center strip disappeared into the most perfectly rounded ass he'd ever seen. Alex rolled his eyes to the ceiling. "You're really killing me, Trouble."

He knew he was a total lowlife, but reached out for her anyway. He caressed one cheek and sighed. Her firm, smooth flesh felt like velvet. His fingers slid toward the honeyed skin of her inner thigh. The damp denim of his jeans barely contained his erection as he recalled an entry in her diary.

She opens her legs, shamelessly watching him watch her. His fingers slide into her wet heat, gliding in a circular rhythm. She arches against his hand, urging him on...

He reluctantly pulled the covers over her and stepped back from the bed as his conscience gnawed at him. There were all kinds of reasons to keep his distance. Not the least of which was she could be a suspect. He'd learned from Emelio's mistake. He ought to stay away from her. He knew better—

Aw, hell. He was going to make love to Meghan.

ALEX LAY ON HIS BACK, tired, spent and gasping for air.

His bare skin was hot and flushed, his hair soaked with sweat. The scent of Meghan's fragrance filled his nostrils. Every muscle in his body ached with fatigue. When he got his breathing under control, he peeled open his eyes to gaze up at her.

Even with tousled hair and no makeup, she still looked beautiful. Despite her bloodshot eyes. "Finished already, Nick?"

Her words floated down to him, barely audible above the pounding of his heart. She had the kind of voice created for telephone sex. Not that a guy like him needed auto-erotic pursuits. Usually.

"Give me a break. I've been at it for the last hour."

He placed the barbell and weights back on the rack and struggled to sit up. Meghan stepped back from the bench press to give him room. He got to his feet and stretched, showing off the results of his labor. The admiration in her golden-brown eyes was worth the effort.

He hadn't slept worth a damn the whole night. But instead of flashbacks to Overtown, images from her journal had kept him hard awake. Every time he tried to slide into unconsciousness, another fantasy stole over him, increasing the aching pressure in his groin. She was all he could think about. Not even a five-mile run and an hour of throwing steel in the gym had burned off his restless energy.

Alex grabbed his towel off the floor beside him, dried his face and chest. A grin tugged at his mouth when he noticed her eyes following his movements. He flexed his biceps, posing for her. "Are you here for one of the exercise classes?"

"Actually, I came for the Stress Release Shiatsu Massage." She rolled her shoulders and took a deep breath, drawing his attention to her breasts. She wasn't wearing a bra today. Seeing her nipples strain against the thin cotton of her T-shirt opened a floodgate of desire.

"Feeling tense, lady? I have just what you need."

"I'll bet you do. But I'll stick with a massage for now."

He latched onto her last two words, lowering his voice to an intimate level. "That leaves all kinds of possibilities for later."

Instead of flirting back, Meghan glanced away. Bright color crept onto her cheeks and she twisted the bracelet on her wrist. He touched his fingers to her shoulder, guiding her toward the bank of windows. "So, Trouble. Where have you been all morning?"

"I've been, um, avoiding you."

"Well. That's brutally honest."

She winced and brushed her hand over his forearm. "Forgive me, please. I'm so embarrassed. Those Miami Vices were pretty strong and I don't normally drink."

Alex leaned one hip against the wall, offering her a sympathetic grin. "Yeah, you were toasted, all right. How's your head?"

"It's still attached, I think." She rubbed her temple and grimaced. "I couldn't swear to it, though."

"Make sure you drink plenty of water—"

"Nick, I'm really sorry about last night."

He concentrated on her eyes, needing to gauge her response to his next question, and braced himself for the answer. "Are you sorry about all of it?"

"What do you mean?"

"Never mind, forget it."

He stared blindly out the window, absently rubbing his chest where his ego had been bruised. If Meghan forgot the most incredible kiss he'd ever had, he sure as hell wasn't going to jog her memory. Here he'd tried to be a gentleman... Well, except for fondling her butt while she lay in a drunken stupor.

"I regret drinking so much and letting Julie set me up with those losers. Mostly, I'm sorry for the way I treated you."

"I wasn't complaining."

"I remember." Her voice was alluring, her tone silky, when she answered. Amusement twinkled in her eyes as she swept her gaze over his body. "Oh, do I remember."

He flinched and looked at her in surprise. Did she wake up last night without him realizing? "Uh, you do?"

"At least, up to a point. We were on the beach and then I was in my room with a killer hangover."

Good. His secret was safe. Alex hesitated for a second, then just had to ask. "So, you also remember what you told me?"

She managed a choking laugh. "How could I forget? I've never done anything like that before in my life. I can't imagine what you must think of me."

Alex cupped her cheek in his palm, looking deeply into her eyes. "I think you're a beautiful woman who recognizes the inevitable."

"I should probably explain. I need to tell you why—" She broke off when someone walked close enough to overhear their conversation.

"Do you still want to go snorkeling this afternoon? We can talk on the way."

"Yes, I want to go. I can meet you at the pier in an hour or so." Meghan placed her hands on his forearms and rose up on tiptoes. She pressed her lips against his in a warm kiss.

The sweetness of it sang through his veins. He smiled, feeling strangely…happy. "See you at three o'clock, Trouble."

Alex watched her walk away, mesmerized by the sway of her hips in the tight white shorts. His eyes followed her across the gym and up the steps toward the spa before he went into the locker room.

He must be losing his damned mind to even consider

getting involved with her. The background check Emelio had done came back clean. No wants or warrants, not even an outstanding parking ticket. Meghan had nothing to do with the cartel. Still, Alex knew it would be a mistake.

Given her attitude about law enforcement, she probably wouldn't hang around if she knew the truth about him. Normally he wasn't one to shy away from a conflict. But until he knew what Ramos was up to, his true identity had to remain protected.

Shit. Here he was in the same old situation again.

His ex-wife, Liz, had divorced him because of the secrets he'd kept and the lies he'd told, the sudden disappearances and the unexplained absences. She had refused to understand that, for Alex, being a DEA agent wasn't just a job; it was the key to his identity.

After stripping off his sweaty tank shirt and drawstring pants, he turned on one of the showers and stepped under the pulsating spray. The hot water hit his shoulders, flowed in rivulets over his chest and down his torso, dripping off of his thighs. He worked up a lather, then began washing the residue from his skin.

He suddenly pictured Meghan on the massage table and wished he could trade places with the masseuse. The image of her lying naked before him and moaning softly filled his mind.

Her tawny skin would be as warm and pliant as silk from his caresses. His hands would grip her shoulders, rub her back, then knead her thighs. He'd lean over to find out how that smooth, soft flesh tasted....

Alex groaned in frustration. He ducked his head under the shower spray to wash his thoughts away along with the shampoo. Turning the shower dial to cold, he stood under the freezing spray until his raging lust was under control.

7

I stare at our reflection in the mirror as Nick cups my breasts. My nipples harden against his palm. I watch my skin warm under his fingers, feel the echoing heat in my belly...

MEGHAN CLOSED HER DIARY and placed it beside her on the sofa. Tucking her feet under her, she stared blindly out the window. She'd never felt so aware of herself as a woman. Her body hummed with the sweetly aching need Nick had aroused in her. Leaning back against the cushions, she closed her eyes.

She brushed one index finger over her mouth. The sensitive skin tingled at the memory of his lips pressing against hers. Her breasts grew heavy as she imagined his large hands gliding over them. She slipped her hand beneath her T-shirt, her breathing shallow, her body tingling.

Gently squeezing the pliant flesh, she stroked her thumb over the erect nipple, eliciting a shiver. She gasped, enjoying the sensation her fingers created. For a moment she considered taking the edge off, but she'd done that too often lately.

Meghan opened her eyes and sighed as she pulled her shirt back into place. A mere fantasy couldn't compete with the desire Nick had unleashed in her. She wanted to use his gorgeous body in the most erotic ways, to make him moan and beg for her touch. Now that she'd tasted paradise in his kiss, she wanted to devour it until this new hunger was satisfied.

Maybe next she'd ask Nick to make some of her fantasies come true. She broke into a self-conscious grin recalling some of the things she'd written over the years. Then again, maybe she wouldn't ask him. Her fantasy life was pretty dynamic, her diary filled with visions she'd never dare tell another soul.

She inhaled sharply, her brows drawing together in a frown.

Meghan looked down at the green paisley diary beside her. She'd written the last entry in the blue one when she arrived at Cayo Sueño. This was her new diary, the one she started after Julie left yesterday.

Where was the old one?

SHOW TIME.

As he waited for Meghan, Alex saw Rogelio Braga get off the shuttle launch from Key West. His stomach clenched against the nausea. Braga recognized him, too, and headed in his direction. Apprehension hit him at the same time as the adrenaline. Alex shoved his hands into his pockets, clenching his fists to still the fine tremors.

I've got this. I'm in control.

He inhaled deeply and struggled to slip into the mask of his cover. Dammit, it shouldn't be this hard to shift gears. He'd played the role before. The persona wasn't an easy one for him, given his physical looks and size, but he had the skills to pull it off. He *had* to pull it off.

Within seconds, "Nicholas Alexander" stood on the pier while his prospective employer approached. Shoulders hunched to reduce his profile, he affected a slick grin and a weaselly attitude. He changed his speech pattern to match his identity, talking faster in an eager tone.

"Señor Braga, it's good to see you again, sir. I was looking for you last night so I could thank you for your generous gift."

Braga took the hand he offered in greeting. His grasp was mild, in keeping with the Latin custom, but still a reminder that power isn't always physical. "It was the least I could do. I'm very pleased that you like the wine."

"I do, Señor Braga. I hope you'll accept my invitation to drink it with me. Maybe when we close our deal?" Alex smiled to show his deference even as he pushed for an answer.

Braga crooked two fingers, indicating they should walk further along the pier. "Tell me, Nicholas. What do you plan to offer Frankie Ramos?"

A bullet through the heart. With effort, Alex pushed aside thoughts of the dead informant, the murdered agent and revenge. He mentally sorted the information he had on file. His reply had to be in keeping with his role as a finance geek, but still further the case.

"There are hundreds of ways to provide the services your organization requires. Before I can give you an answer, I'll need to know more. Such as where different assets are located, how they're currently transferred. Then we can discuss what avenues are available and which ones can be explored.''

''Vagueness has its place and, while I do appreciate your discretion. I need for you to be candid. What can you do that our other bankers have not?''

''Nick Alexander'' was being tested. Braga's intense expression revealed the importance of his answer. *Go for it.* Alex decided to admit some of his knowledge of the cartel's operations.

''Your small-scale thinking has to be replaced with a global mentality, señor. Turning small dirty bills into boxes of large denominations takes time, space and risk. Moving actual cash out of the country in private planes is—''

''Unsophisticated.'' Braga shook his head, as if criticizing the stupidity of this, though he didn't voice the opinion. ''It does, however, allow us to maintain some privacy regarding our financial transactions.''

Alex nodded, trying to act like he was anxious to earn the ten percent commission the cartel would pay his brokerage firm. ''Keeping the government out of your business is vital. There are some exemptions from the currency reporting laws. Loopholes, if you will.''

''I will, as soon as you tell me how.''

Bright yellow. The color caught Alex's attention and he glanced over Braga's shoulder. Meghan was strolling along the pier toward the ferry. She hadn't spotted him yet, but it was only a matter of time.

''I am not a man who forgets a favor. Or a slight.'' Braga smiled thinly.

Alex flicked his gaze back, alerted by the nuance in Braga's voice. *Concentrate on the job, the girl can wait.* ''You have too much money here in the States. That capital needs to be released into the international banking system. That's where I come in.''

Braga laughed, appreciating his obvious bid for inclusion. ''If you can bring our laundering operations into the twenty-first century, you will take part in the organization's future. I will see to it personally.''

His tone was casual. Not so the look in his eyes. Braga obviously had big plans—Alex didn't need it engraved and hand-delivered. The head of the Miami cartel, Frankie Ramos, was going down and Braga planned to push him under.

MEGHAN SEARCHED the marina for Nick. She caught sight of a tall, dark haired man and assumed no one else would wear that ugly bright orange-and-green floral shirt. Or fill it out so well.

He stood talking with a familiar-looking Latino man. She couldn't see their faces, but their body language seemed a bit clandestine. Wondering about the odd scene, she watched them shake hands before the other man walked away.

Nick seemed preoccupied when she approached. That wouldn't do at all. Giving in to a naughty impulse, she reached around to pinch his rear. He started, looking down at her in wide-eyed amazement. Then his surprise gave way to amused pleasure. She shrugged unapologetically.

''I couldn't resist.''

''You're starting early, Trouble.''

He'd called her that last night as well. In the Foster family, she'd always been the good girl. He only used the term to tease her, but Meghan still got a little thrill from hearing it. She finally had a cool nickname.

"So, what were you and that guy talking about?"

"Who?"

"Brava? Brana?" She searched her memory for the man's name. "Braga, that's it."

Wariness flashed in his eyes, but vanished so quickly she might have imagined it. "Just passing the time while I waited for you."

"Really? It looked kind of serious to me."

After the slightest hesitation, he admitted, "Señor Braga is the client I told you about."

She narrowed her eyes and her voice took on a hard edge. She really hated being lied to. "Last night in the lounge you acted like you didn't know him."

"That was Braga? I didn't recognize him."

She wrinkled her brow in disbelief. Then she thought back. Señor Braga *had* left before Nick came over to her table. "Oh. I guess you didn't."

"Are you ready to go?"

He handed her aboard the ferry that would take them out to Dry Tortugas National Park. Nodding toward the stairs, he met her gaze with a sensual smile. "Do you want to be on top or underneath?"

"I like it on top."

The kaleidoscope in his eyes shifted and carnal heat leapt between them. "I'll keep it in mind, Trouble."

A warm sexual glow spread over her body, settling between her thighs. Meghan laughed even as her pulse sped up. Apparently his joke had backfired on him.

Thoughts of him never seemed to leave her mind. She'd become obsessed with the idea of getting naked with him. Top, bottom or sideways, she wanted Nick in the worst way.

She climbed the steps and chose two seats towards the front of the boat. Leaning back in her chair, she kicked off her sandals and propped up her feet. He crossed his long legs and rested his deck shoes on the lowest rail. His thighs, bared by his denim shorts, were perfectly shaped with lean, hard muscle. Her fingers itched to reach over and stroke them.

As the ferry got under way, one of the crewmen came by offering refreshments. Nick ordered a beer for himself. "You should probably stick to juice today."

She stuck her tongue out at him and ordered a cola. After pushing her sunglasses onto her nose, she took off the bright yellow shirt covering her swimsuit. Meghan stretched her arms above her head and sighed. Her headache was gone, her stomach had settled and she was with Nick.

"It's a beautiful day, isn't it?"

"Yeah, the view's real nice." His eyes slowly took in her skimpy bikini top. She felt his heated gaze brand every inch of flesh not covered by the neon-purple material.

"I like what I see, too. Except for the shirt, of course."

He took a swallow of his beer and pretended to frown. He glanced down at the repulsive orange-and-green fabric, then back at her. "You have no appreciation of quality fashions."

"Yes, I do. That's why I hate your shirts." Desire coiled in her belly as she admired the dark gloss of his disheveled hair, the laughter in his eyes and the natural sexiness of his smile. What might have happened last night if she hadn't passed out? The prolonged anticipation of being with him was like one of the fantasies she'd written.

I wait in suspense for the dangerous pleasure of his touch. He whispers softly in my ear, telling me of his desire, his need and his love....

Wait a minute. That reminded her. She'd searched her luggage but hadn't found her blue diary. Meghan toyed with the soda can, careful to use a nonchalant tone. "By the way, Nick. Did I leave anything in your suite?"

"Don't think so." He stared down at the deck and reached for his beer. "What are you looking for?"

She didn't want to tell him too much. The part of herself she expressed on those diary pages was very personal, intensely private. "Um, nothing of value to anyone but me. I can't find a particular book."

"Maybe the resort's gift shop has another copy. You could just replace it."

"No, it's... Never mind. It's an old one, anyway." Meghan reluctantly dismissed her concern. The diary would turn up. Right now, she wanted to just relax and enjoy the day.

The sky was a brilliant lapis and afternoon sunlight glinted off the blue-green water. Above the rumble of the boat engines, frigate birds cried as they spread their seven-foot wings to glide on the updrafts. The mild trade wind carried the scent of brine along with the spicy fragrance of the Creole lunch buffet.

Nick reached for her hand, rubbing the back of it with his thumb. The movement sent little tremors racing along her nerves. He gently tugged her fingers until she looked over at him. "Your proposition was a new experience for me. I got the impression it was new for you, too.''

"It was." She glanced away and back again. "I don't want you to think that I come on to every guy I see."

"Glad to hear it." His smile was all male arrogance. "Is that what you wanted to tell me earlier in the gym?"

"It's about last night, about the way I acted." She hated talking about Rob and the crotchless panties, but an explanation was in order. She didn't want Nick to judge her by her outrageous behavior. "My ex-boyfriend decided he wasn't cut out for monogamy."

"How did you find out?"

She ducked her head, old hurt rising to the surface. "I found some underwear that wasn't mine. That made it kind of hard for him to deny he was cheating."

"He sounds like a moron. Not because he didn't deny it—because he cheated on you in the first place." Nick set his empty bottle on the deck beside him. "So, what's this have to do with last night?"

"I felt so betrayed, so angry. The whole sordid thing really affected my self-confidence."

He lightly squeezed her fingers, but said nothing. His quiet understanding soothed her. She didn't need alcohol to boost her courage this time. This time she could say the words with bold confidence.

"I want to prove that I'm not cold or uptight, so I've decided to take a lover. I want *you* to be my lover."

She saw the heat flare in his eyes just before he raised her hand to his lips and kissed it. "And I want to be yours. You're beautiful and sexy and I know we'll be great together."

"I've never felt sexy or desirable. Until I met you and you made me feel—I don't know—like nothing I ever felt before." Meghan dropped her gaze. This was so embarrassing. "Rob said that I never satisfied him. But then, he left me completely unfulfilled, too."

Nick dipped his head to peer at her intently. "Are you telling me you've never had an orgasm?"

"He was the only— I mean, I've never been with— Oh, never mind. I only wanted you to understand."

"Don't worry, I do. When you're ready, I'll be gentle and take my time. All night, if necessary." He winked and gave her that grin she adored.

"Are you bragging or flirting this time?"

"Bragging. Definitely bragging."

All night. Oh, wow.

She was thrilled that he agreed to her proposition, but needed to clarify what they were getting into. For the first time in her life, she had control. She could give as much or as little as she wanted, without worrying about letting someone down. This was her chance to be impulsive and make her own needs a priority. If she set the rules, she wouldn't get hurt.

"I want to make it clear that this will just be physical. A week of sexual exploration with no strings, no promises and no regrets." She looked at him squarely. "Agreed?"

"There's no such thing as 'just sex,' Meghan. Every encounter, no matter how casual, has an effect on the people involved."

She tilted her head. "I'm surprised to hear this coming from a guy. I thought women needed a reason for sex and men just needed opportunity."

As Nick's eyes searched her face, his expression revealed a tenderness she wasn't prepared to deal with. "I'll agree to a satisfaction of mutual needs and desires. But you have to agree to be open to whatever happens between us."

She hesitated. He could be talking about uninhibited sex or falling in love. She'd come to Cayo Sueño with the intention of shedding her prim and proper insecurities. But she hadn't counted on meeting someone who excited and intrigued her; a man who could matter if she wasn't careful.

"All right, Nick. You've got a deal."

WHEN THE FERRY DOCKED on Garden Key, he suggested touring Ft. Jefferson first. She listened absently while he read aloud from the brochure, something about the Civil War-era coastal fort becoming a national monument in 1935. Who cared?

Her mind was whirling with questions. When? Where? How many times? And her body hummed with excitement. A flutter of nerves accelerated her pulse as a thousand possibilities raced through her mind. *Omigod. We're really going to do this.*

She followed Nick to the visitor's center to rent masks, snorkels and fins. An electric current of awareness zinged through her every time their eyes met. When she reached for his hand, the smile he offered was ripe with promise. They walked to the beach on the west side of the small key.

Meghan dropped her tote bag onto the chalk-white sand, then kicked off her shoes and peeled down her shorts. After coating her skin with sunblock, she drank some water and turned to offer Nick the bottle. The words died on her tongue.

Who would have guessed what was under those ugly shirts?

Her eyes roamed hungrily over his wide shoulders, powerful arms and broad chest. When he stripped off his shorts, her gaze moved to his flat stomach and heavily muscled thighs, admiring the way his swim trunks clung to his rear.

"Ready, Meghan?"

"Yes, I am." She was more than ready. The seductive, husky tone of her voice made him grin as he showed her how to use the snorkel. She was intensely aware of him, this big strong male who turned her on just by breathing. A delicious pressure grew in her belly, making her thighs tingle. He really was perfect.

Diving beneath the waves, she marveled at the sight that appeared. The turquoise waters off the rocky shoal exposed a world teeming with marine life. Vibrant sea fans swayed in the gentle current. Bright sponges and staghorn coral rose from the sandy floor.

She watched Nick cut through the water a few feet ahead. His strokes were powerful, confident as he followed one of the endangered loggerhead turtles for which the Tortugas was named. If his strong, sure movements were anything to go by, he was going to be incredible in bed.

Coming up for air moments later, she treaded water under the bright sun. Then suddenly she felt Nick's large hand sliding up her thigh. She took a deep breath just before both hands grasped her waist and pulled her under. He held her, weightless beneath the waves, as schools of boldly patterned fish darted about in a blur of yellow, black, green and blue.

They'd been swimming for about an hour and

Meghan hated for the experience to end. But her legs were tired and the sun had burned her back and shoulders. She found her footing in the shallows and pushed the mask onto her forehead.

Nick broke the surface a moment later. He took off his snorkel and walked up beside her wearing a grin that mirrored her own. His eyes gleamed as he looked her over. She glanced down to see the wet nylon clinging to her hardened nipples.

She laughed shyly. "I guess the water's a little cold."

"Let me warm you up."

He moved in close, one strong arm around her waist and the other draped over her shoulder. She reached up and wound her arms about his neck, pulling him even closer. His kiss was raw, primitive, the action of a man claiming a woman as his own. He took her mouth with a savage passion and she returned the kiss with reckless abandon.

A wild flash of pleasure raced through her body as their tongues met and mated. He made a rough, impatient sound in his throat as he molded his pelvis to her belly. Only two thin strips of nylon separated his burgeoning erection from her tingling center. She arched against him, rubbing, teasing. He shuddered and tightened his grip.

Slowly, Meghan became aware of sounds other than those of the wind and waves. She reluctantly broke the kiss and opened her eyes. Her cheeks flamed with embarrassment when she finally recognized the whistles and laughter of a dozen or so onlookers.

"We've got an audience."

"They're just jealous. Walk with me." Unmistakable desire smoldered in the depths of his green eyes. She was immensely pleased she had that kind of effect on him. Heaven knew he turned her on like a switch.

Holding Nick's hand, she strolled beside him along the powder-soft sand, skirting the waves that rolled gently up the beach. The incoming tide was a dull roar broken only by the cries of gulls overhead. Sunlight sparkled on the water and the occasional seashell that washed onto the shore.

He led her over to the shade of a stand of palms, and eased her down onto the cool sand. She felt a surge of excitement when he gathered her into his arms. A heavy, aching need settled in her belly, making her tremble with desire. She clung to him, their bodies as close as could be without becoming one.

"I'm going to fulfill that beach fantasy of yours."

She tensed, startled by his words. "How do you know about that?" Did he have her old diary after all? That's the only way he could—

"You told me last night, remember? At the party."

"Oh. Yes, I did. Right before you kissed me senseless."

He laughed. "I think you were senseless from those drinks, but thanks for the compliment."

"It was you, Nick." She met his gaze boldly. "Do it again."

"My pleasure."

He teased her lips apart with his tongue, his mouth slanting across hers again and again until their breath came in harsh gasps. A delicious shiver ran through her and the touch of his hand to her breast increased the hot ache.

The evidence of his passion pressed against her leg. Nick moved his hand to massage the tender flesh of her inner thigh. Questing fingers delved under the edge of her swimsuit. Meghan arched closer to the seductive torture. She spread her thighs, opening herself to him and anything he wanted to do with her.

Her eyelids fluttered but she refused to close them. She watched his face, saw the male arrogance in his expression as he pushed one finger, two fingers, inside. His thumb circled her clitoris, urging her on, making her desperate for release. A flame of desire ignited within her, burned away all inhibitions.

A whimper escaped her throat as he increased the erotic pressure. She arched against his hand in wanton abandon, bit her lip to keep from crying out. The slow, insistent throb became a deep pulsing tremor until she thought she would die from the pleasure.

Now she wanted him fully inside her. Meghan reached for his swim trunks, tried to free him from the restraining fabric, but Nick leaned back slightly. When she tried again, he pulled away.

"Why did you stop? I was so close…" She saw her own hunger and longing reflected in his gaze.

"I know, I know." He struggled to get his own breathing under control. "But your first time shouldn't be on a federally protected beach."

She tried to pull him back into her arms. "I'm not a virgin—"

"It's *our* first time. Let's make it special."

"Nick, I don't want to wait. I can't wait."

"If I can, you can. Be mine tonight. Let me show you how good it can be."

ALEX SAT out on the balcony of his suite, reading the last couple of entries in the journal. This thing was pure gold. A priceless window into the mind of a fascinating, contradictory woman. While Meghan was sweet and conservative, "Elise" was a hedonist who indulged in the wildest of desires.

As he read, he jotted some notes on a sheet of the resort stationery. Interestingly, it seemed like every entry she'd written was a fantasy. Some were just fun, others sensual. The rest were hot enough to singe the page. Inhibition was limited only by imagination.

But he noticed she never seemed to write about anything true, anything real. Her journal was filled with fantasies, but no memories or anecdotes. It was like she didn't want to face whatever held her back.

How could a woman so hot, so receptive to sensual pleasure, think she was cold and uptight? It was obvious she'd never given herself over to the ultimate ecstasy. But if she let him, he could show her that, by surrendering, she would actually triumph. They both would.

He couldn't shake his disappointment over the boundaries Meghan had set. He wanted to explore a relationship, not just sex. She drew him in ways he couldn't understand. There was something about her that made him feel alive. He wanted… He had no idea what he wanted. But she'd made it clear she was just looking for a good time.

It was for the best. Now was the wrong time to get involved. As it was, he should be checking in with Brent, not planning a romantic evening of seduction. Too much depended on closing this case for anything more serious to develop with Meghan. It would distract him from his job.

He shifted in his seat, trying to relieve the pressure straining his zipper. Hell, he was already distracted. He had Trouble on his mind. Meghan had awakened feelings he'd shoved aside years ago. He wanted her. After only two days, it was that simple and that complex.

Alex picked up the stationery and looked over the list. "Rent a tuxedo… Buy condoms… Do the strawberry thing… Let her take control…"

He got up to call her and to make the arrangements. He was going to return Meghan's journal tonight. Then he intended to bring every one of her fantasies to life.

8

I touch my body, enticing and teasing and pro-
voking him. Boldly sensual, eminently sexual, I
weave a spell of lust. For once, I am not myself
but the darker side of me.

MEGHAN STEPPED into the elevator, her stomach quivering with sudden anxiety. A combination of hope and
fear made her heart beat an unsteady tattoo in her chest.
What should she anticipate? What did Nick expect of
her? She wasn't exactly an expert on casual sex.

*It'll be okay. It will be better than okay. It will be
fantastic.* She stared at her reflection in the mirrored
walls of the elevator, trying to see herself through
Nick's eyes.

Julie had loaned out the contents of her closet again.
Thin satin straps crossed over her bare shoulders to the
beaded trim of her dress. The single yard of royal blue
material scarcely covered her breasts and ended at the
middle of her thighs.

Her skin felt hot, heightening the color in her cheeks.
Her parted lips appeared soft and moist and red.
Smoke-blue shadow made her eyes look wider than
usual, emphasized the sparkle of excitement. The

woman in the mirror looked like the alter ego from her diaries. She looked wild, wanton.

She looked like a woman who was about to get laid.

Meghan Foster, Sex Goddess in Training. She winked at herself as the elevator doors slid open onto the eighth floor. Head high, shoulders back, she sauntered down the hallway to suite 809. Funny about fate. If she hadn't checked into the wrong room, she never would have found the right guy.

She'd barely knocked before the door swung open. *Oh, wow.* Nick stood tall and relaxed, sure of himself and his rightful place in the universe. He radiated an innate vitality that attracted her like a moth to a flame.

He wore a black tuxedo that fit his body as though tailor-made. The open jacket revealed a blue, green and white floral vest. The snowy linen of his shirt contrasted starkly against his olive skin. A pair of black western boots and the diamond stud gracing his left earlobe offset the elegance of his attire.

The man gave sexy a new definition.

Suddenly she was in his arms. Meghan shut her eyes and breathed in the scent of his skin. She could feel his heart pounding in time with hers. She brushed her fingers along his jaw down to the hollow of his throat and into the open collar of his shirt, exploring the differing textures of his skin.

His fingers caressed the sides of her face as his mouth captured hers, urgent and demanding. His hands were everywhere at once, sliding, squeezing, stroking. When he sucked her tongue deeper into his mouth, she felt the pull all the way down to the apex of her thighs.

With a soft groan of reluctance, she broke the kiss so he could close the door. No need to shock the neighbors. If that kiss was anything to judge by, she was in for an incredible night. She was ready, more than ready, for her sexual adventure to begin. Meghan clutched her evening bag a little tighter and nervously headed toward the bedroom.

"Not so fast, Trouble." Nick caught her hand before she could take another step.

"I thought— Um, aren't we—?"

"Yeah, we are. But we've got all night. First, I had a special meal sent up for us. Come into the living room."

The scent of fresh flowers and spicy candles filled the room. Romantic music floated from the radio, blending softly with the breeze whispering through the open doors. Out on the balcony, a table was set with crystal, china and more candles. A rolling cart sat next to the rail.

While Nick dimmed the lights, Meghan dropped her purse on a chair and stood in the center of the room, waiting. His approach was that of a dangerous animal barely held by an invisible leash. The very air seemed electrified.

The look in his eyes was wild and hungry as he stalked toward her. His mouth curved into a devastating smile, the kind a predator would wear. Her instinct was to run for her life. Her desire was to throw herself into his arms and beg him to fulfill her darkest fantasies.

His gaze never left her as he took her fingers. He turned her hand and then pressed his mouth to the sensitive spot on her wrist. Her pulse beat riotously against his lips and she knew that if she ran, it would be toward him.

Nick held out his arm and turned her around in a

slow circle. His eyes focused on her face, then slowly took in the length of her body. "You look ravishing tonight, Ms. Foster."

"You look like just the man to ravish me, Mr. Alexander." She hardly recognized her own voice. "Could I possibly convince you to skip right to dessert?"

He looked tempted for a moment, then shook his head. Tucking her hand into his elbow, he guided her out to the balcony. After seating her, he took the other chair and removed one of the covered dishes from the cart.

"Nick, I don't have a plate, or any cutlery."

"You won't need them."

He lifted the lid and chose a dark black olive from a crystal bowl. Holding it lightly between his fingers, he reached out, a devilish grin on his handsome face. She leaned forward to take the glistening olive between her lips. When she extended her tongue to lick the brine from his fingertips, his pupils dilated in response.

Clearing his throat, Nick poured a glass of champagne and held it for her. The taste of the wine burst on her tongue like the tang of ripe grapes. He turned the glass and drank from the same spot her mouth had touched. The heat rose in her face as she watched the intimate gesture.

He continued to feed her bite after bite of cheese, Gulf shrimp, fresh-baked croissant and backfin crabmeat. She sucked his fingers after each morsel, enjoying his unguarded reactions. She'd once written a similar fantasy, in which her lover catered to her culinary whims before satisfying her sexual ones. How wonderful to have life imitate art.

Nick chose a large strawberry and knelt before her. As he spread her knees, his thumb stroked hot circles inside of her thigh. The other hand trailed the berry along the opposite thigh. Then he bent his head to lick the sticky red juice from her skin.

He placed the berry between his parted lips, lifted his head to hers, leaning forward. She met him halfway and pressed her mouth against his. He bit the fruit in half and its essence ran over her tongue. She wasn't sure which was sweeter, the strawberry or the taste of his kiss.

One type of hunger had been satisfied, but another kind was growing inside her. Something powerful and overwhelming that made her breathing shallow and her pulse rapid. She sat back in her chair and stared down into Nick's green eyes.

"Soo...what's for dessert?"

"Anything you ever wanted...or dreamed of wanting."

She gasped softly, taken aback by the seriousness of his tone and the intensity of his gaze. His voice was filled with both temptation and promise. Feeling light-headed, Meghan realized she was holding her breath. She slowly exhaled as she fought an unexpected urge to cry.

It was perfect. *He* was perfect.

Nick had no idea what he was offering her, or how badly she wanted to accept. She trusted him but suddenly felt afraid. Could reality possibly measure up to her wildly vivid fantasies? There was no doubt in her mind that he would be a fabulous lover. It was herself that she doubted.

"It's been a while. I hope you understand if..."

Alex placed a finger against her lips. He was surprised to see apprehension steal over her features. He figured she'd be eager to live out the scenes in her journal and get "crazy naked," as she'd put it last night.

"It's okay, Meghan. Whatever happens is okay. Whatever doesn't happen is okay, too."

The tension vanished from around her eyes and she gave him a sweetly seductive smile. Her voice was soft, husky with emotion. "Make all of my dreams come true tonight, Nick."

Still kneeling at her feet, he dropped his chin, briefly closing his eyes. "Nick." How ironic that he had to keep playing a role in order to get her to stop playing one. He wanted to be himself, wanted her to be with the real Alex. Just as he wanted to be with "Elise," the real Meghan.

"I can't do that unless you keep your part of our bargain. Be open and adventurous tonight. Let go and show me the darker side of you."

For a second, her brows furrowed in confusion. She must have recognized his choice of words from her diary. Damn. He'd better watch it until he could return the book and explain why he had it. His mistake almost broke the mood.

"All right, Nick. Tell me what you want."

"No. Tonight is for you. Just for you. All I ask is that you trust me."

What he really wanted to do was sweep everything to the floor and take her right there on the table. Instead, he stood up and held out his hand, giving her the choice of accepting it.

Meghan didn't hesitate to reach for him. Her small

hand felt warm in his as together they stepped through the door. He let go of her just long enough to take off his tuxedo jacket and drape it over the armchair. Then he guided her over to the couch.

He gathered her onto his lap, pulling off her shoes. He wrapped one arm around her waist and caressed her bare thigh with his other hand. He breathed in the spicy floral scent of her as she leaned close to loosen his tie.

After opening the top buttons of his shirt, Meghan rained sweet little kisses along his jaw and throat. Sliding one hand behind his neck, she stroked her fingers through his hair.

"I want you, Nick. In every possible way."

Every possible way? Images from her journal flashed across his mind. It was going to be one hell of a night.

The first brush of her soft lips against his mouth whetted his appetite. The second touch had him wanting to devour her. Her kisses were tentative, teasing, and he met each one with a restrained passion. Finally, finally she deepened the kiss, her tongue exploring his mouth in lazy circles.

Then she got up from his lap and stood before him. With a wicked gleam in her eyes, she reached behind her back and slowly unzipped her dress. The blue fabric slid off her body, trickled to her feet. His mouth went dry as he stared at her strapless bra and matching black thong panties.

"I've been fantasizing about that set since I saw it in your luggage."

Those tiny excuses for underwear may as well have been spray-painted on. His fingers wouldn't know the difference between the satin of the material and the satin of her gorgeous flesh. The candle's light cast a warm glow over her, creating shadows and shades of tiger's eye and gold on her skin.

He ached to explore everything from the dampness of her invitingly parted lips to the smooth skin along her back, from the velvety softness of her breasts to the slick, wet passage between her thighs.

His awareness of every detail of her heightened. He saw the pulse in her throat, seeming to echo the beating of his heart. He watched her breasts quiver as she breathed. He noticed the tightening of her abdominal muscles, the unconscious sway of her hips.

"Are you planning to stare at me all night?" Her lips parted softly in a smile. "Or are you going to touch me?"

Lust heated his blood until he felt like his whole body was on fire. He wanted her so badly it hurt. But passages from her diary held him in check.

Freedom to give only as much as I want and take as much as I please... I choose to be with a man who makes my pleasure a priority, not an afterthought...

"Believe me, Trouble, I plan to touch you. And taste you as well. Just show me where."

The tone of her skin on her face changed, deepened as her blood warmed. She was clearly embarrassed by his request, but the yearning in those beautifully expressive eyes devastated him. Lord, what a woman.

"Show me," he urged.

She lifted her right hand and placed long elegant fingers against her lips. He leaned back on the sofa cushions, showing her the proof of his desire. The bulge in his tuxedo trousers strained against the material.

"Where else?"

Meghan raised her eyes back to his face and trailed her fingers along her chin and down her neck, while her left hand began to caress her right arm. When she ducked her head shyly, he did his best to reassure her.

"You're safe with me. I won't do anything you don't want. I won't touch you anywhere you don't ask."

After a few seconds, she raised her chin. Boldly looking into his eyes, she skimmed both hands across her breasts. She rubbed her nipples with her thumbs until they tightened visibly against the fabric of her bra. Then she slid her hands lower, along her belly toward those little panties.

Alex's brain shut down as her fingers moved to massage her hips and thighs. Then slowly, Meghan widened her stance and slid both palms up to the apex of her endless legs. When she caressed the satin material covering the gate to paradise, he pulled her to him. "Get over here."

She straddled his lap, her laughter turning into a gasp when he ripped off her bra and flung it aside. Her gasp became a moan as he cupped her naked breasts with both hands. The soft orbs just filled his palms, warming beneath his touch. Her nipples lengthened as he rolled them between his fingertips. As he gently squeezed and stroked, a sexy whimper escaped her.

Sliding his fingers down her arms, he manacled her wrists and drew her hands behind her back. He leaned her slightly away from him until he had unlimited access to those pretty breasts. Meghan shivered at the first touch of his lips, instinctively rubbing herself on his lap.

He kissed every millimeter of her right breast before

sucking the pert nipple into his mouth. Her little sighs and murmurs were making him crazy. He eagerly anticipated the sounds she'd make when he finally sank his flesh into her.

"Omigod."

She gasped, then pressed her left breast insistently to his lips. Following her unspoken demand, he licked that nipple before suckling it against the roof of his mouth.

"Take off your shirt, Nick. I want to feel you against me."

He let go of her wrists and tore open his shirt, not caring when the buttons scattered across the sofa. He drew a shaky breath as her fingernails raked through the coarse hairs on his chest. She lightly grazed his nipples until they were as hard as her own.

While he freed his arms from the sleeves, Meghan leaned forward to bite his earlobe playfully, sending another wave of need to his groin. Alex wrapped her in his arms, molding his lips to hers. She tangled her fingers in his hair and pulled his head closer, deepening the kiss as his hands followed the curve of her bare ass.

Her mouth was hot and demanding, her movements a little frantic. When she reached between their bodies to gently squeeze his penis through his trousers, he wondered how he would explain a stain to the dry cleaner.

He shifted her until she was cradled in his arms and then stood up. She draped her left arm about his neck and kept kissing him as he carried her into the bedroom. Softly backlit by the table lamp, she lounged invitingly on the bed. Waiting. For him. An unfamiliar possessiveness gripped him by the throat, making speech impossible.

When he joined her at the edge of the bed, she got to her knees, wrapped her arms about his waist. His hands slid up her beautiful body to cup her face between his palms. Her whiskey-colored eyes gazed into his with quiet trust.

"I need you, Trouble. Let me love you."

She blinked, and he wasn't sure which of them was more startled by his slip of the tongue. She stared into his eyes for a moment, as if searching for something.

"Give yourself to me now, Meghan, and I swear you'll never be sorry."

Surprise and a sudden sheen of tears filled her eyes. Alex brushed his lips across her forehead, understanding. What started as a game to bring her out of the journal and into his arms now had deeper meaning and far more risk. He was asking her to show him a part of herself she'd never revealed before. He was asking her to open her heart.

He gently kissed her temples and cheeks before softly claiming her mouth. His left hand caressed the tender skin along her jaw as she parted her lips beneath his. He slid his other hand to her breast, his palm slowly caressing the soft mound until the nipple beaded again.

Her hands slipped past his waist, her long nails lightly raking over his hips to his butt. He twitched when her fingers danced over his skin. "Ticklish, Nick?"

Now both hands sought to torment him, causing him to strain forward until his erection pressed against her abdomen. He reached around to still her hands, then leaned down to nibble a sensitive spot below her ear in revenge.

She shifted to one side, rubbing her cheek against the hair covering his chest. Then she captured one flat brown nipple between her lips. Alex groaned as she sucked and licked the hardened bud. With his hands occupied restraining hers, he could only give in and enjoy the erotic sensations.

When she gently bit down on his vulnerable flesh, a bolt of pure lust shot straight down to his groin. He claimed her lips once again, kissing her with all the passion he felt inside. He tasted her excitement and responded in kind.

Moments later, she leaned back to look at him, the expression on her face faintly amused. The gleam in her golden brown eyes was pure mischief. "Those are very nice shorts. I happen to be quite fond of silk boxers."

He crossed his arms defensively. Busted. He wasn't about to admit how much he liked the feel of the slick material sliding over his bare skin. Guys just didn't talk about what they wore under their jeans.

"As nice as those boxers are, they'd look better on the carpet."

Alex laughed. "Oh, yeah?"

"Yes. It's only fair. I stripped for you."

"Okay, Trouble. You asked for it." Imitating a classic bump and grind, he slid his shorts over his hips, then stopped and turned. Glancing over his shoulder with a lascivious grin, he tugged the silk material off one cheek, then the other.

Meghan whistled her encouragement. "Take it all off, baby!"

Alex pivoted to watch her face as his underwear slithered down his thighs and pooled around his ankles. An arrogant smile spread across his face. The obvious appreciation in her expression reminded him of a deer caught in the high beams of a truck. So okay, he was bragging, but she hadn't blinked in a really long time.

The expression of enjoyment on her face shifted to one of need. She breathed his name on a moan and reached for him. The muscles of his shoulders and stomach tensed as he anticipated the first brush of her fingers on his hard flesh. He gulped in a draught of air when he felt her soft fingers wrap around his penis. She held it just firmly enough for him to feel his pulse against her palm.

And then she moved her hand. Her fingers slid over the length of his shaft and cupped his testicles. Her fingers left a trail of fire wherever she touched him. He couldn't possibly get any harder. Then she moved her hand again. He trembled with a need so fierce, it was all he could do to hold back.

He fought for control as she stroked him, getting more confident, more brazen, as she watched his reactions. She was obviously proud that she could bring him to the edge like this.

Hello, Elise.

When she slid off the bed onto her knees, a light sweat broke out on his skin. She leaned toward him, a wicked smile playing on her full red lips. Her tongue extended from between her lips, and she touched the very tip of it to the very tip of his penis.

He gasped and arched his hips forward, but Meghan grinned and backed out of reach. Over and over, she pleasured him with nothing but the briefest flick of her tongue. He thought he'd lose his mind from wanting more.

She looked up, coyly tilting her head. "Do I have to tie you down to keep you from wiggling?"

The very thought of being restrained for her pleasure damn near sent him over the edge. He knew his voice sounded strained and a little desperate. "Save the kinky stuff. We can play Mistress Elise and her Love Slave some other time."

"Mistress. Elise." She tilted her head, her brow furrowed as she regarded him. "Where did you come up with that?"

"Your luggage tags. Can we talk about this after you—"

She took him completely into her mouth. Alex shuddered and threw his head back, his fingers tangled in her short curls. When she made humming noises in the back of her throat, he was close, so close to losing it.

He shut his eyes and thought about baseball, tax returns, crabgrass…anything except how fantastic her lips felt around him. Another minute of oral sex and he'd finish before he got started. As much as it pained him to leave the warmth of her mouth, he wanted to see to her pleasure.

This was supposed to be *her* night. He drew in a ragged breath as he pulled away and raised her to her feet. After laying her on the pillows, he tugged off her panties and lay down beside her.

He gathered her into his arms and felt her heart pounding against his chest. Her warm, soft curves molded to the contours of his body perfectly. Holding her, he was shaken by the sense of rightness. Like that second of anticipation just before lightning strikes, he was standing at the edge of a precipice.

Years of undercover work had trained him to use his head, suppress his feelings. He'd always held a part of himself back. He had to. But with Meghan it was different. He was different. He wanted to be a part of her life, to become a part of her and she of him. The power of his emotions left him both stunned and disoriented.

Damned if he wasn't falling in love.

9

He takes me quickly, takes me roughly, takes me over the edge. I face his passion and equal it with my own.

SHE WAS ON THE VERGE of internal combustion, and Nick wanted to cuddle. This wasn't exactly the frenzied sex scenario she'd envisioned. Meghan grabbed a handful of his tush, urging him forward. His leg hairs tickled her inner thighs when he shifted. She shivered with anticipation when he positioned himself between her spread legs, supporting his weight on his elbows.

His large body pressed hers into the mattress. Far from uncomfortable, she welcomed his weight. He kissed the sensitive column of her throat and arousal shot her pulse into overdrive. She uttered a frustrated groan and wiggled her hips. She'd never before felt this hot, this ready, so fast. If he didn't take her soon she would... She'd bite him.

Frenzied with need, she clutched his shoulders and rubbed against him. She couldn't get close enough. She wanted him inside her. The waiting was going to make her insane, she just knew it. Ducking her head into the hollow of his neck, she nipped his collarbone.

"Ouch! What was that for?"

"Touch me, taste me, take me. Now!"

When she arched against him, his erection grazed her clitoris. Her breasts were heavy and aching for attention, the nipples hard against his chest. Burying her fingers in his soft, wavy hair, she pushed his head lower.

He didn't need any more encouragement. She groaned as he enthusiastically suckled her nipples and licked her breasts. When he trailed his open mouth down her chest and over her ribs, she discovered new erogenous zones. His sharp teeth gently nibbled her belly in revenge as he moved farther down her body.

Meghan half gasped, half moaned at the first touch of his mouth to the damp, swollen flesh. She'd never let anyone do this before. She wiggled and squirmed until he finally looked up, gripping her thighs tightly to keep her still.

"You asked me to taste you." His voice was rough-edged with desire. "Now lie back and let me."

She relaxed and lost herself in the sensations his wickedly clever tongue created. Her hips began to move against his mouth, dictating the rhythm. His strong hands imprisoned her as she quivered in response to his intimate attention.

"Oh…yes." Her breath came in harsh gasps. Her body strained for release. Her fingers flexed, tangling in the damp threads of his hair, holding his head in place. When his tongue delved inside her, her whole being caught fire and a familiar tightening began in her belly.

She'd felt this tingling, tugging pressure before, but never with a partner. The joy of it almost brought tears to her eyes as Nick coaxed her toward a quickly escalating climax. She couldn't think, she could only feel, as she shuddered with the most incredible orgasm she'd ever experienced.

Meghan lay panting while she returned to earth, both relieved and amazed at her body's response. She wanted to feel this way forever. Opening her eyes, she saw a smug grin tugging at the corners of his damp mouth.

"Wow. That was... Wow."

"We're just getting started, Trouble."

His tone was filled with male arrogance, like he'd just conquered Mt. Everest. He looked so proud of himself that she couldn't resist teasing him. She feigned a cynical expression, raising one brow and turning down the corner of her mouth.

"You can't possibly do better than that."

"Is that a challenge?"

Nick lunged forward to capture her lips in a hot, greedy kiss. Raw hunger built inside her as she explored his mouth. The first orgasm had only increased her desire. Tickling his ribs, she used the element of surprise to flip herself on top of his sexy body. Pinning his wrists over his head, she returned his smug grin.

"You're at my mercy now, mister, and I intend to have my way with you."

She trailed her fingertips along the skin inside of his forearm. Her hands slid from the column of his long neck over the wide expanse of his shoulders to the heavy muscles of his biceps. She caressed the flat, well-defined planes of his abs before moving on to his narrow hips and hard, toned thighs.

Beneath her hands she sensed his leashed strength and knew that he was indulging her. For now. Gazing into his light green eyes, she saw both tenderness and challenge. Meghan acknowledged the subtle power play, knowing that in the end they'd both win.

Nick raised himself up, trying to capture her left breast in his mouth. Maneuvering just out of reach, she reveled in the frustration on his face. Joining their hands so the fingers interlocked, she forced his arms back over his head.

This time he lay passive, watching her. She liked the way his eyes crinkled when he smiled, the heat of his gaze as he looked at her. She brushed her lips against his, seducing him with her tongue. He tasted of cinnamon; he tasted of her.

She leaned over to lick his neck, then gently blew on the wet spots. Nick shivered beneath her but remained still when she rubbed her breasts over his chest. She felt every muscle in his body go taut and a groan escaped his throat in a slow, ragged breath. A light sweat covered their skin where their bodies touched. The heat building between them was enough to scorch the sheets.

Without releasing his hands, she eased her lower body toward his lap, watching his face while her damp flesh slid down his belly. He lifted his hips and his rigid shaft made contact with the tiny bud of flesh at the core of her need.

Meghan rubbed herself along his length, intensifying the pleasure and prolonging their satisfaction. His entire frame vibrated beneath her. Then he whispered a single word, his voice hoarse and darkly sensual.

"Mercy."

She experienced a sense of power as old as Eve, realizing she could affect a man this way. Even more exhilarating was knowing she affected *Nick* this way. It looked like her training was over. She was a real Sex Goddess now. Triumphant, she began to take him inside her. Instead he gently broke her grip on his wrists and eased her aside.

"Wait. Gotta get something."

Reclining on her elbows, she laughed out loud when she saw the label on the box in his hand. "A thirty-six pack of extra large with sensation ribs? You really believe in being prepared."

"I got them for you."

She tried to snort in disbelief but the feel of his warm, clever fingers caressing her was a wonderful distraction. She opened one of the foil packages and tossed the wrapper aside. "Lie back. I read this in a book once and always wanted to try it."

He stiffened when her teeth scraped his vulnerable flesh, then groaned in surprised delight as she unrolled the condom onto him using only her mouth.

"You're killing me, Trouble."

"Don't the French call an orgasm *le petit mort*—?"

"No more talking."

With one arm about her waist, Nick flipped her over and nestled his body between her spread thighs. She arched her back when he entered her slick passage, her body adjusting to the way he stretched her, filled her.

Crying out in need, in relief, the pleasure of his possession overwhelmed her. He began rocking his hips in a deliberate, sensuous rhythm that she quickly matched. Then he drew his knees closer, slowed the pace, changed the angle of penetration.

"Open your eyes, Meghan. Look at us."

He levered himself onto his elbows and she raised

her head to watch. It was incredibly erotic to both see and feel their bodies join and separate. Again she experienced the wondrous aching, the quickening in her belly.

He must have felt it too because he accelerated the tempo, increased the glorious grinding pleasure. Wild and wanton, she reveled in his hard, fast thrusts. Wrapping her legs tightly around his pistoning hips, her hands clutched at the sweat-slick muscles of his back.

"More. Please." She barely recognized her own voice as she urged him on.

"Everything I have, sweetheart."

He growled the promise while shifting his body slightly. Nick reached his right hand between their sweaty bodies until his thumb found the catalyst that intensified her enjoyment. He rubbed and stroked the nub of flesh in languid circles. At the same time, he plunged himself deeper, again and again.

The orgasm shuddered through her, rocking her to the core. Her vaginal muscles clamped down on him, contracting almost painfully against his large size. A sensual wave crested over her, followed by tremors of ecstasy.

Eyes closed, his features tense, he moved faster, pushed harder. She felt the telltale pulsating inside her that preceded his climax. Holding her like the only anchor in a storm, his whole body stiffened. A triumphant groan escaped his throat when he found his own release.

After a few mind-numbing moments, she felt her soul return. Breathing hard, Nick still lay buried inside her. Meghan closed her eyes, tried to catch her breath.

Too overwhelmed to speak, she was filled with a sense of gratitude, elation and wonder.

She'd hoped for amazing sex, but the emotional intensity had caught her off guard. It was probably a side effect. She'd opened herself—literally—to the most intimate contact possible. Of course she would feel a little poignant afterward.

The important thing was not to get caught up in it.

"No. No!"

Meghan jerked awake at the sound of an angry shout. Her heart thudded in her chest. For a moment she was disoriented, her eyes struggling to focus and make sense of the darkness.

"Don't do it..."

The words were cold, razor-sharp. The harsh tone made her shiver. She raised herself on one elbow and looked over at Nick lying beside her. Moonlight shone through the bedroom window onto his face. His amicable charm was gone, replaced by a hard mask. His jaw was clenched, his brows drawn together in a scowl. She jerked away from what she saw, not recognizing the man she'd just had sex with.

"Michael Collins in Jackson..." He muttered the name under his breath as he stirred restlessly in his sleep. "Andy Ruiz in El Paso. Nick... Alex..."

She leaned a little closer, reached out tentatively to pat his shoulder. "What? Who are you talking about?"

"Sorry, Greg... So damned sorry..."

Her fear dissipated when she heard his remorse. She smoothed the frown from his brow, comforting him. When her fingers skimmed over the thin scar dividing his left eyebrow, he flinched at her touch.

"My fault… Should have… Sorry, Greg…"

She draped her arms over him, embracing him tightly until he settled down. He murmured softly, unconsciously nuzzling his cheek against her hair. After a few minutes he seemed to fall back into a peaceful sleep.

Wide-awake, Meghan lay beside him, absorbing his agitated heat. She continued to hold him, wondering what dreams plagued his rest. Everyone had nightmares occasionally, but the change in his demeanor was shocking.

Who was this man she'd just given her body to? She'd met him two days ago, hardly knew him at all. Suddenly, it was like he had a split personality. Meghan huffed out a breath. Then again, so did she. Perhaps she wasn't the only one escaping into a role during this vacation.

Nick's breathing slowed, indicating deep sleep. She eased away to relieve the numb tingling in her arm. Looking out the window, she saw the full moon had drifted lower in the night sky. She needed to go. She wanted time alone, to think and to sort out the emotions churning her up inside.

As wonderful as it had been, having sex with a total stranger now seemed like a mistake.

Meghan rolled off the bed, eager to avoid the awkwardness of waking up in his arms. She located her panties behind a chair and hastily pulled them on. In the bathroom, she winced at the sight of herself in the mirror.

The lovely ringlets of the night before were now the tangled curls of the morning after. Her lipstick was smudged, her foundation had vanished and sapphire shadow circled her eyes, making her look like a raccoon.

She grabbed a cloth to wash her face and borrowed Nick's hairbrush to repair as much of the damage as possible. Out in the living room, she put on her bra and dress, not bothering with her shoes.

Meghan checked her evening bag for the card key inside. How humiliating it would be to get locked out in last night's formal wear. She cracked open the door, peering into the hallway. No insomniacs. Easing the door closed, she headed for her own suite.

Years of writing about intimate and uninhibited encounters didn't prepare me for the real thing. Nick is an incredible lover and being intimate with him was like discovering a new world. Or maybe I simply discovered myself and what my body is capable of.

In my fantasies, though, I didn't feel altered in some elemental way. My dreams have been totally sexual, with no emotional commitment. Nick touched me—ME. And I'm not sure how I feel about that.

ALEX WOKE UP ALONE. Not an unusual occurrence. But the sense of abandonment was completely foreign.

The bed sheets were cool with only his body to warm them. He rolled onto his stomach and cuddled the pillow against his chest. The scent of Meghan's calendula body oil still lingered. He closed his eyes and laid his cheek on the case.

He was acting like a high-school kid with his first crush.

Lying there contented, he waited for her to come back to bed. And waited. Finally, he went to find her. The living room was empty and so was the bath. His brows drew together, his lips thinning with displeasure. When the hell had she left?

Why had she left?

Dejected thoughts accompanied him into the shower. He'd done his best to recreate her fantasies. He'd tried to make their night special. And she'd just up and left, without so much as a "thanks, it was fun."

He'd chosen the food based on what she'd written. He'd recreated her game of "show and taste." He'd let her set the pace of their lovemaking. He'd restrained himself in order to fulfill her dream. How the hell could she have just sneaked off into the night after that?

The seduction had affected him more than he'd expected. How could he give a woman her first orgasm, during the best sex of his life, and *not* fall in love? But she'd left. She'd just left!

He had no right to feel cheap and used. Meghan told him up front what she wanted from him. But, dammit, he'd never been loved and left before. Alex slammed the faucet shut and stomped, dripping wet, to the telephone. He dialed her number, waited in annoyance for her to answer.

"Morning, Trouble."

"Hi, Nick. Um, did you sleep okay?"

The caution in her tone warned him. "I guess so… Why?"

"You must have had a bad dream. You kept apologizing to someone named Greg?"

Oh, shit. Not last night, of all nights. Alex sat on the arm of the couch and let out his breath in a slow hiss.

The psychologist had warned him that he'd be more vulnerable to the nightmares when his emotions ran high. The telephone line was quiet while she waited for an explanation.

"Greg was—is my younger brother. I, uh, haven't seen him in a while." He wondered, not for the first time, whether Greg was even still alive. Guilt weighed on him. His brother was the reason he needed to get back to work and stop pursuing a woman who only wanted his body.

"Oh, I'm sorry, Nick. What—"

"Why didn't you wake me before you left? I'd planned to start the day off right and make love to you again."

She hesitated, as if she wasn't sure how to answer. "I thought we were finished. I mean, I thought we had our night of hot sex...."

The awkward pause was a stab in his heart. Was this how women felt the morning after? "We're not finished, Trouble. Not by a long shot. You agreed to be open to whatever happened between us."

"I did. Last night was fantastic. But we're on vacation. This is only an interlude before returning to our real lives."

His many "real" lives marched across his memory and he knew she was right. But he couldn't settle for mindless coupling, even though that's what *he'd* agreed to. Keeping Meghan out of his business wouldn't be easy, but he'd find a way to keep her in his life.

"Give me the rest of the week to be with you."

"Nick..."

"I want to have an affair. And I want all of the courtship and intimacies that go with it."

"Why start something that will be over in a few days?"

Good question. Ninety-nine percent of the male population would be thrilled to have a woman offer "no strings, no promises, no regrets" sex. He was a complete idiot.

He closed his eyes and let his voice convey his feelings. "There's a kind of magic between us. Don't bother to deny it, especially not after last night. Let's explore it and see how far it takes us."

She was quiet for so long that he braced himself for her refusal. Finally he heard her draw a long breath. "All right, Nick. I'm yours. For the rest of the week."

Well, it was a start. After agreeing to spend the day together in Key West, she hung up and Alex went to get dressed. He grabbed a cigarette, pinched off the end and went out to the balcony with her journal.

He'd sincerely intended to return it either last night or this morning, whichever presented the best opportunity. Now, though, he decided to read through the whole thing again. He needed to fully understand what made Meghan tick.

It was the only way to show her that reality beat fantasy every time.

10

_____

Elise throws back her head, uttering a throaty laugh. She is slick with need, restless with desire. Her dark lover enters her with one quick thrust and she comes almost immediately.

ALEX GREETED MEGHAN with a smile and leaned down to brush his lips over hers. At first she didn't react and his heart lurched at the rejection. Then she returned the kiss, hungrily exploring his mouth with her tongue, and his world settled back into place.

Damn. He had it bad.

"Nick, that has to be the ugliest one yet."

He looked from her teasing expression down at the large red, white and green pattern on his shirt. "What are you talking about? This is a great shirt. I wear it at Christmastime."

She draped her arms behind his neck, pressing the length of her body against his. "Festive or not, it's still ugly. I'll just have to take it off of you."

"Oh, yeah?"

"Yes." She brought her lips right to his ear and whispered, "And I'm only going to use my teeth."

Then she'd trail her hot mouth down his naked chest until she undid his jeans the same way... Alex placed a hand on either of her hips, holding her against the hard-on she'd created. "Now you're going to have to stand in front of me until I can walk again."

"Gosh, what should we do while we're waiting?" She slowly rubbed her pelvis over his zipper, making the situation worse.

"Cut that out, Trouble."

"Aw, what's the matter, Nick?"

"I'm about to get arrested for public indecency, that's what." He dipped his head to nibble the side of her neck. "You're going to pay for this later."

"Mmm, my pleasure." Meghan flicked her tongue across his lower lip. Then she pulled back and offered him a bright grin. "You know the city, so where should we go first?"

Thumbs in the belt loops of his jeans, Alex discreetly adjusted himself. He cleared his throat and tried to get his brain working again. "The Key West Aquarium is right at the end of that pier. How about we start there?"

She made a face. "After seeing all of those cute fish, I won't be able to eat their relatives. You promised me seafood for dinner, remember?"

"Okay. Let's go to Mel's place then. You'll like all the girl stuff there."

"Girl stuff?"

"You know. Gold, pearls, rubies…"

"Ooh, that kind of girl stuff." She rubbed her palms together in glee.

Inside the Mel Fisher Maritime Heritage Society Museum, Alex spotted a sign outside the small theater. A short documentary about *La Nuestra Señora de Atocha* was about to start. The seventeenth-century galleon sank off the Marquesa Keys in 1652. After a long search, Fisher and his crew finally salvaged the *Atocha* and its priceless treasure.

If Alex remembered right, the film was about fifteen minutes long. He pointed to the theater entrance. "Let's go over there."

"Oh, that looks interesting."

"I think you'll enjoy yourself." He was formulating a plan in his mind. *Paybacks. You gotta love 'em.*

There were no seats left, but that worked in his favor. He led her to the back corner of the theater as the lights dimmed. Standing close to the wall, he drew Meghan in front of him and whispered in her ear.

"No matter what I do, you can't make a sound."

When she nodded tentatively, he moved his hands up to her breasts, cupping their weight in his palms. Meghan looked around, obviously afraid someone could see them, but he didn't stop. He gently pinched her nipples until they hardened through the fabric of her tank top.

Her breathing was shallow, excited, as the film flickered over her face. Eyes half-closed, she leaned her head back against his shoulder. Then he slid his right hand down the front of her shorts. He heard her quick intake of breath in the darkness and smiled.

"Not a sound, remember."

After a few seconds, she relaxed and widened her stance. His fingers rubbed lazy circles around her clitoris before dipping into her moist heat. A soft breath escaped her parted lips as her body tightened around his fingers. He pushed deeper, making her wiggle against his hand.

She was hot, she was wet and she was at *his* mercy.

Alex brushed his lips over her ear. "I'm so damned

hard right now. Can you feel me? I want to be inside you, moving faster and deeper until you come screaming.''

She was on the edge, breathing hard and biting her lip. He glanced at the screen, and with impeccable timing, removed his hand just as the credits rolled and the house lights came up.

Meghan blinked, eyes wide in her flushed face. She turned, hiding from the departing crowd, and exclaimed under her breath. ''Oh. My. God. I can't believe you did that.'' She whacked his chest with her hand. ''I can't believe you stopped!''

He tilted his head to steal a kiss. ''I told you I'd pay you back.''

She groaned aloud and thunked her head on his chest. ''You're horrible, Nick. Absolutely monstrous.''

''Want to finish the tour?'' Laughter seeped into his voice, but his jeans were damned uncomfortable right now.

''You think you've won, don't you? This isn't over between us, mister.''

''Glad to hear it, Trouble.''

Back out in the museum, they wandered hand-in-hand through the exhibits. Slipping her arm around his waist, Meghan stared in wonder at the displays from the *Atocha*. ''I can't imagine spending sixteen years looking for this shipwreck.''

''If you want something bad enough, you don't give up on it.''

She glanced at him with a slight smile before returning her gaze to the seventy-eight-carat emerald Fisher's crew had found. ''I'd say all of this was worth the wait.''

At the end of the tour, Alex bought a small Spanish coin from the gift shop. "For centuries this lay at the bottom of the ocean. When it was finally found, it was a black misshapen lump. Now look at it."

"It's beautiful."

"It's for you." He gazed intently into her eyes as he handed her the silver real. "You have to work slowly and carefully to reveal what's underneath something before you see the true value."

She angled her head to one side. "I get the feeling you're talking about more than a Spanish coin."

"Wouldn't want you to overlook a priceless treasure."

"I understand, Nick. But we don't have sixteen years; we have four more days. My vacation ends on Sunday."

He reached for her hand, stroking his thumb across the back. "It doesn't have to."

"Yes. It does. I don't have any experience with one-night stands, but—"

"What do you mean, one night?" He pulled his hand away. "You gave me the rest of the week—"

Meghan placed one finger on his mouth to stop his instinctive protest. "Let's just live in the moment and enjoy our time together, okay?"

He agreed. But he wasn't giving up, either. He wanted her to acknowledge that the feelings they'd shared in bed still connected them. The sex was incredible, but more than that he enjoyed the laughter and the friendship. He enjoyed *her*.

Back outside, the midday sun glared off the sidewalks and heated the air until it sweltered. As they strolled down Duval Street, Meghan playfully swung his arm back and forth. "Key West is so cool! I mean, just look over there. There's a T-shirt place beside an elegant gallery next to a seedy-looking bar and an exclusive dress shop."

"Yeah, I really like it here. The best part comes later, while the sun goes down."

She smiled eagerly. "What happens then?"

"You'll see. It's a pretty unique experience."

"Oh, look! I want to go in there." Meghan dragged him into Unmentionables, a small boutique specializing in lingerie. Like a kid in a candy store, she led him from one display of intimate wear to another. "These little mesh briefs almost match your favorite shirt."

He stared at the blue-and-orange underwear, pretending to be insulted. "No way would I fit into those things."

"No, I guess you wouldn't." She glanced at his zipper, then picked up some very short, bright-green silk boxers. "Why don't you model these for me?"

"Here? I don't think so."

"You can try them on later. We'll play the Ambitious Actor and the Casting Director." When she leered and wiggled her eyebrows suggestively, he burst out laughing. More and more, the real Meghan was shining through.

"Nice addition to my theme games." He pointed toward the back of the shop. "What about that studded leather outfit? It would look great on Mistress Elise."

Her expression turned mischievous. "That's right, I threatened to tie you down last night, didn't I? Let's go look at the toys on the back wall. My love slave needs—"

"Forget it, Trouble." He refused to move when she

tried to tug him through the aisles. "Sorry I brought it up."

After making a few purchases, including the boxer shorts, Alex showed her the Audubon House and the Old City Hall before heading for the Truman Annex, the late president's vacation home.

Noting the angle of the sunlight, he glanced at his watch. Shit. He'd lost track of time. Emelio was meeting him outside of the DEA's Post of Duty Office in half an hour.

Meghan saw the gesture and teased him about it. "Are you tired of my company?"

He turned with a smile and took her into his arms. The slow sweetness of the kiss turned hard and hungry until they were both breathing heavily.

"Did that feel like I'm tired of you?"

"Not at all. So what's your hurry to leave?"

"I'm supposed to hook up with an old friend—"

Bang! The air suddenly exploded with sound.

HER HEART SLAMMED to a stop. She felt the blood drain from her face as she fell. She dropped into a crouched position, dragging Nick down with her.

"Meghan."

Her fingers trembled on his arm. Keeping her head low, her eyes darted around, looking for the shooter.

"Meghan. It was just a car backfiring."

Nick's commanding tone finally broke through her panic. He wrapped his arms around her, helped her stand. The warmth of his touch didn't offset the cold immobilizing her. She couldn't meet his gaze, couldn't catch her breath to speak. He settled her on a wrought-iron bench under a huge banyan tree, then slid onto the seat beside her.

She tilted her head back, hugging herself as she stared at the twisted trunks reaching more than thirty feet toward the sky. Inhaling deeply, she felt her cheeks flame. *This is totally embarrassing. He must think I'm crazy.*

Nick kept silent, giving her time to pull herself together. Then he leaned forward, resting his elbows on his knees. "Talk to me."

Her pulse still raced, but the warmth returned to her hands. She cleared her throat, swallowed back the tears. "I told you my brother-in-law was a cop, right?"

"Yeah. You mentioned it."

"Well, he got shot. And I was to blame."

He jerked his head around, his expression a mix of curiosity and disbelief. "What happened?"

She remembered it so clearly, like a horror movie she'd watched over and over. Her throat ached as she forced the words past. "Julie and I were waiting in the car for Kyle to get sodas at the convenience store. Then Jules decided she wanted ice cream, so I went inside.

"When he saw me, he whispered for me to leave. I remember he sounded angry, but I also heard his fear. Then I realized he wasn't even looking at me.

"Up at the checkout counter, a dirty-looking guy was pointing a gun at the cashier, hissing at her to hurry. She was frantically emptying the register. The guy's voice sounded desperate. I remember how badly his hand shook. It was obvious the kid was high on something."

Her voice hitched and Nick reached for her hand. "It's okay. Take your time."

"I grabbed Kyle's arm to get his attention. I reminded him that he was off duty, that Julie was still in the car. I begged him to leave with me and call for help. Kyle said he couldn't wait, that just because he hadn't punched the clock didn't mean he could ignore a crime in progress."

Tears welled in her eyes, spilling over onto her cheeks. Nick gently stroked his thumb across the back of her hand, encouraging her to go on.

"One minute I was arguing with him, the next I was lying on the tile. He'd shoved me down to reach for his gun. I looked up in time to see that horrible red starburst appear on his white shirt. I'll never forget the sound of the gun blast, Kyle crying out as he fell. And that smell, that sweet coppery stench."

Nick's light green eyes shifted, darkened with some unknown emotion, but his tone was calm and sympathetic. "It must have been awful for you. But I don't see how it was your fault."

"If I hadn't been arguing with him, if I hadn't distracted him—"

He cradled her chin between his fingers and shook his head. "Kyle was a cop. He knew the risk. Blame the guy who robbed the place, not yourself."

Logically, she knew he was right. And Julie had long ago absolved her. But she would always feel responsible. She took a deep breath, tried to lighten the mood. "Now you know more about me than I wanted you to." She looked up at him through lowered lashes. "Can we talk about something else, please?"

"There's something you should know. I meant to tell you last night." He stared at her, a somber look on his face. She held her breath, alerted by the seriousness of his tone. "I don't know how to tell you this...." His words trailed off. He was obviously struggling to get them out.

"What is it, Nick?"

He blinked, a slight frown tugging at his mouth. After a moment, he ducked his head. "I'm afraid of spiders."

"What?" She was confused by his bizarre confession.

He slapped one palm against his thigh. "I knew it. I knew you'd lose all respect for me if I told you."

"What makes you think I respected you before?"

The easy grin spreading across his face was dazzling against his olive skin. He opened his arms to her. Grateful to him for making her smile, Meghan went readily into his embrace. She leaned into him, allowing his strong shoulders to support her. *I wish—*

She stopped the thought cold. It was stupid to want more than was possible. She was the one who'd made the rules, after all. After her father left, she'd carefully mapped out her life. Knowing where things stood and what should happen next made her feel secure. Her feelings for this man would lead her down a totally unfamiliar path.

Nick turned her whole world upside-down. Everything about him tempted her to open her heart again. But if she lowered her defenses, she'd only get hurt when they went back to their real lives. She dried the last of her tears and pulled a brochure from her bag.

"Where to now? I'd like to go see the Curry Mansion. The owners have turned it into a guest inn, but we can still tour the museum."

Nick winced as he checked the time again. "Actually, I need to meet my friend."

"Okay. We can all tour the house together."

As they walked along Front Street toward Whitehead, she glanced toward him and noticed that a shadow darkened his features and his expression seemed tense.

"Why don't you go ahead? I'm not into antiques and old houses."

"I kind of wanted to see this place. But we can go somewhere else—"

"No." He smiled to soften the effect of his words. "I don't want you to miss it. Let's split up for a while and then the rest of the day is ours."

He was trying to ditch her. She finally interpreted the look on his face. Insecurity gnawed at the edges of her newfound confidence and she wondered about the gender of Nick's "friend."

Well, what did she care? They hadn't made any promises. They didn't have any kind of committed relationship. So what did it matter if he met a friend instead of spending time with her? It didn't. Not at all.

Meghan forced a pleasant expression, trying to keep the jealousy out of her voice. "If I didn't know better, I'd think you don't want your friend to meet me."

He touched her face when they stopped in front of the white three-story Victorian estate. "The truth is I don't want *you* to meet him."

"Why not?"

"Because you'll take one look at Emelio, fall madly in love and dump me like a hot rock."

Meghan tried to match his attempt at levity. "Well, then, I've got to see this guy—"

"Nope. Go enjoy yourself. I'll come back for you around two o'clock, I promise." He kissed her before turning to leave.

She watched Nick stride away, feeling let down. Ridiculous, since they were supposed to be nothing more than sex partners. But the rules were shifting subtly out of her control.

The touch of his lips had been brief, but the effect of it stayed with her. His kiss had carried traces of tenderness and possession and…complications. She was fully aware of the attraction between them. Magic, he'd called it. She felt it, but resisted giving in to it.

Meghan climbed the steps to tour the mansion built in 1855 by Florida's first millionaire. She wandered though the high-ceilinged rooms, admiring the Tiffany glass windows, well-preserved antiques and ornate décor.

An hour or so later, she stood on the widow's walk plucking at her fuchsia tank top. From here, she had a view all the way to the water, but the slight breeze rustling the tree limbs had no effect on the humidity. After snapping some photos, she turned to go downstairs where it was cooler.

A blur of red, white and green caught her attention and she recognized Nick's shirt. He stood on the corner about one block up Caroline Street. He and his friend were having a discussion that involved a lot of agitated hand gestures and accusatory finger-pointing.

If Meghan guessed accurately, their conversation wasn't a pleasant one.

"HAVE YOU LOST your effing mind?"

Emelio's voice was laced with disapproval. "You're

telling me that instead of leaning on Braga, you spent the night with some piece of ass?''

Alex shot him a vicious glance, letting loose his own anger. "Don't *ever* refer to Meghan like that again."

"I can't believe you'd jeopardize our case like this. Come on, Alex. Didn't you learn anything from my mistake?"

"This is different, Em. She's different—"

"If Brent finds out you're chasing some woman instead of Ramos, he'll pull us off this assignment before we can kiss our badges goodbye."

Alex slid his hands into his pockets and frowned, defiance warring with uncertainty. The bottom line was that something finally meant more to him than the job. "I can't explain it, hombre. We only met forty-eight hours ago and—"

"And it's too damn soon to know if she's worth destroying your career." Emelio studied his face. Whatever he saw had him reaching for his cigarettes. After lighting one, he tossed the packet over. "We're running short on time, man. Easton has my pager number on speed dial."

Alex pinched the end off the cigarette. He inhaled deeply, welcoming the nicotine rush. "Have you found Ramos?"

"You'd know if you were helping me with this damned investigation."

He took the hit, knowing he deserved it. "Have you found him or not?"

Emelio huffed out a breath. "He's lying so low he's not even casting a shadow. On the plus side, the monitors we put on the local banks have paid off. We've been able to identify and flag some of Ramos's deposit accounts.''

"Excellent. Now to figure out how the cash is coming in and which offshore banks he's liquidating it to.''

"That's where you're supposed to come in. Think you can focus long enough to handle it?''

"Back off, Em.'' Alex let his voice take on a cool edge.

His partner pushed anyway. "Keep your mind off this woman and let's get it in gear, man. No evidence means no indictments and no jail time.''

"I hear you, I hear you.'' He ground the cigarette out with the toe of his boot, then picked up the butt to throw into the trash. "I've got to go and meet Meghan.''

"Looks like she's meeting you.'' Emelio nodded his chin, his gaze narrowed beyond Alex's shoulder. "Her driver's license photo didn't do her justice. She's really hot.''

"Watch it, Emelio.''

His partner looked back at him. "How do we play this?''

"I met an old friend.'' Alex turned and Meghan waved in greeting as she walked up.

She stood on tiptoes to plant a warm kiss on his mouth. He couldn't help but grin. Just being near her sent ripples of pleasure through him. Every time their eyes met, he felt a warm, heavy ache in his chest.

Yeah. She was worth it.

"Finished touring the house already?''

She pointed over her shoulder in the direction of the Curry Mansion. "I saw you from the roof and thought I'd come over to introduce myself.''

Alex glanced down the street, careful not to let his reaction show. Shit. They'd been careless about meeting in the open. If Braga had seen them, he would have recognized his partner for sure.

"Hi! You must be Emelio." Meghan reached out to shake his hand. "You're even better-looking than Nick said."

With a startled chuckle, Emelio closed his hand over hers then looked at Alex. "I like her—she has good taste."

"That why she's with *me,* hombre."

It was ridiculous to feel jealous. He draped his arm over Meghan's shoulders anyway. She slid her hand down his back, her face all innocence as she patted his butt.

Nope. Nothing to worry about.

"So did you guys have a chance to catch up?"

Emelio shoved his hands into his khakis and forced a smile. "Yeah, it was great to see Nick and rehash the good old days."

"Really? From where I stood, you looked pretty intense."

Alex knew enough to recognize the slight tightening around his friend's eyes. Not only had Meghan seen them together, but she'd guessed the nature of the conversation. Em was going to give him a raft of shit about this later.

He lied smoothly in an effort to throw her off. "It's an old argument about a bet and a practical joke."

"Now there's a story worth hearing." She glanced up at Alex and back to Emelio. "Why don't we all go somewhere and you can tell me about it?"

"Thanks for the offer, Meghan, but my cruise ship

is only in port for the day. I've got to get back." Emelio turned to bare his teeth and offer his hand to Alex. "Good to see you again, *buddy*. Keep in touch."

The grip was crushing and Alex tried not to wince. Em was seriously pissed. "Take care, *pal*. I'll talk to you soon."

Meghan exchanged goodbyes with Emelio before he walked away, supposedly heading for the cruise ship pier.

"Well, Nick, where should we go next?"

His eyes followed his partner down the street. He'd better make things up to Em. His partner had been doing all of the work these past two days. First, he needed to hook up with Braga. Next he needed to push for information about—

"Nick?"

Alex looked down at Meghan, concentrated on her question. "Whatever you want to do is fine."

"Let's go back to the resort, then. I need a nap. After."

"After what? All we did was sightsee, eat and shop…" His voice faded away when she wrapped her arms around his waist. She slowly rubbed her breasts over his chest, then bumped her hips once against his thighs.

She spoke slowly and distinctly. "The nap comes *after*."

11

The blindfold feels strangely erotic as I wait eagerly for my lover's touch. He comes to me in darkness, in silence, intent on possessing me, body and soul....

"I DIDN'T THINK you could move this fast." Meghan struggled to keep pace as Nick pulled her from the elevator.

"We'll slow down when we get to your room. Otherwise, I'll take you right here in the hallway."

Her body reacted to the rough timbre of his voice, but she laughed at the outrageous suggestion. Even Elise wouldn't have sex in public. Oh, wait. They'd sort of done that in the museum. Meghan grinned. She was definitely a bona fide Sex Goddess.

Once they reached her suite, Nick started unbuttoning his ghastly floral shirt before the door even closed behind them. She strode past him, yanking the tank top over her head as she went. In the bedroom, he flung his boxers to the floor next to his jeans and her denim shorts. Her panties landed in another pile with his socks and her bra.

Gleefully naked and crazy with need, Meghan threw her arms around his neck. Her hands fisted in his hair while his mouth claimed her lips. His kiss sent hot flames of desire zinging through her body.

"Now. Right now," she demanded.

When she tried to get to the bed without breaking her hold on him, their legs tangled. She stumbled toward the dresser but Nick put out a hand to brace her fall. Then he looked down and his lips curved into a seductive smile. Her gaze followed his to the silk scarf under his fingers. He slowly lifted it, a devilish gleam in his eyes.

"There's something I'd like to try, if you're not afraid."

Meghan inhaled sharply. Was he thinking what she thought he was thinking? She'd written a couple of fantasies about mild bondage, but never dared to try it.

"Well? Are you?" He drew the material leisurely over his palm, then twisted the ends around his fists.

A wild excitement filled her as she glanced from his face to the scarf. Would Elise try it? Oh, yes. In a heartbeat. The sense of forbidden longing was a complete turn-on. She cocked her head and rested a hand on one naked hip. "Do I look afraid?"

"You look incredibly beautiful." His eyes, clear and intense, glowed with an inner fire. Admiration and something unfathomable mingled in his expression. Nick draped the scarf in front of her face, surprising her by tying it securely behind her head.

She closed her eyes beneath the fabric, unnerved by the sudden heightening of her other senses. The air between their bodies was charged with anticipation. His large hand stroked her hair, his touch light and reassuring, but he didn't speak again.

The silence was electric. She breathed in the soap-

and-water smell of his skin when he swept her into his arms. For a moment she was disoriented as he carried her across the room. He laid her down on the cool bed sheet, then moved away.

Wearing nothing but the blindfold, she suddenly felt vulnerable, exposed. Meghan draped her arms over her waist. She crossed her legs and uncrossed them again. Finally she forced herself to relax. Eagerly awaiting whatever happened next, her heart hammered in her chest.

Unable to see, only to feel, she became acutely aware of the sound of her own breathing, the dampness between her thighs, the soft breeze billowing over her naked body. It was so much like what she'd written—the darkness all around, her lover ready to possess her body and soul—familiar and yet different.

The mattress dipped under Nick's weight and she sensed him shift toward her. When he placed a hand against her shoulder, she startled at the unforeseen touch. She identified the faint smell of cinnamon and waited for the taste of his lips.

His mouth was hot, his kiss soft and drugging. Her entire being focused on his lips and tongue, the only place their bodies met. The heat of his kiss sent flames of lust straight to the juncture of her thighs. A moan escaped her throat.

Then suddenly he retreated, leaving her frustrated. Her earlier inhibition completely disappeared. She reached out blindly, searching for him, desperate for him. Not hearing a sound and fearing he might have left the room, she knew a second of alarm, alone as she was in the utter darkness.

Fantasy and reality merged, intensifying the thrill of

the unknown. Then some primal instinct told her of his presence. She pictured him, motionless by the bed, silent and smug. A smirk tugged at the corners of her mouth. He wanted to watch? She'd give him something to watch.

"Elise" brought her hands up to her breasts, kneading the soft flesh and pinching her nipples. Her skin felt hot beneath her fingers. She stroked her hands lower, letting them slide down over her body. Her fingers moved between her legs and she touched herself the way she wanted him to touch her.

Nick growled deep in his chest, giving himself away. She laughed, low and throaty, realizing she'd been right. The blindfold was supposed to put her at a disadvantage. Yet she'd managed to wrest control from him by indulging her true self.

In an instant, his hand covered hers, both guiding and encouraging her movements. She moaned when she felt his fingers delve inside her. The rush of trembling heat his touch created sent her hurtling toward release. Then Nick pulled both of their hands away, denying her satisfaction.

"Oh, please, I—"

She smelled the heady scent of a rose just before sensing the silky petals against her lips. Almost as soon as she felt it, he moved the bloom away. Then the velvety petals caressed her knee, her hand, her throat. Meghan quivered with impatience, not knowing where the rose would touch her next or when his fingers would replace it.

Nick trailed the flower over her shoulder and along her arm, then over her right breast. Her nipple puckered at the silky touch and excitement rippled in her belly as he took the other one in his mouth. She reveled in the feel of his lips and tongue and teeth against her sensitive flesh. Her body ached for him, for a different kind of touch. The rose, now warm from her heat, glided along her abdomen to the dewy flesh between her thighs.

He followed the flower's path, leaving gentle, moist kisses in its wake. A guttural cry escaped her as she arched her hips to meet his mouth. His lips ravished her hungrily and she reveled in his expertise. Then he stopped again, playing a game of exquisite torture.

''Nick!''

''Shh. You're not ready.''

''Yes, I am!''

''Shh.''

Her belly quivered as rose petals fell like summer rain onto her bare skin. Then Nick covered her, surrounded her. The smell of sweat and shampoo mixed with the scent of the flowers. She spread her legs and wrapped her ankles behind his knees.

His penis lengthened, hard against her delicate flesh. She pressed her mouth to his throat, her hands gripping the hard muscles of his back. His heart pounded in rhythm with her own as his ragged breath warmed her face. Her body wept in preparation of his claiming her.

The sudden tensing of the muscles in his arms and thighs was her only warning before he plunged himself into her. His first thrust had her gasping. The next had her crying out his name. After that, she could only call on the supreme deity.

Passion built within her like a storm while she heaved beneath him, moaning and whimpering. She lifted her hips, crying out at the power of her climax.

He slipped his palms under her, pulling her closer still, and groaned his release.

Tremors rocked his body in the aftermath and the room filled with the sound of their labored breathing. As she caught her breath, a sense of peace and contentment came over her. Eventually, Nick lifted his weight, rolling her with him until he lay under her on the tangled and sweaty bed sheet.

He removed the scarf from her eyes, drawing it over her head before dropping it to the floor. Meghan blinked against the light. Then his beautiful mouth caught her attention. After tracing the outline of those soft, full lips, she leaned down to give him a tender kiss.

Relaxing in his arms, her ear against his chest, she could hear his heart thundering. She felt him whisper something into her hair, but couldn't make out the words. It didn't matter. The message in his embrace was unmistakable.

Nick had imprinted himself on both her body and her heart. Her instinctive response to him was too powerful, the emotions too strong to question. As incredible as it seemed, she was helpless to deny the obvious.

I'm in love.

She couldn't even begin to describe how she felt. It was as if she was feeling it for the first time. *I love Nicholas Alexander.* Instead of being satisfied after the intimacy they'd shared, she wanted more. She wanted forever.

ALEX LEANED one hip against the railing on his balcony, smoking his third half-cigarette, not caring that it defeated his effort to quit.

He'd left Meghan a note saying he needed to change clothes for tonight and would pick her up at seven o'clock. Then he'd spent the next couple hours hunting in vain for Braga. It made him damned uneasy that his contact had become as elusive as his boss, Ramos.

He dragged on the cigarette impatiently. His focus was totally divided between duty and desire. Meghan deserved better than what little he could give. He wanted her to be a part of his life. But what the hell did he have to offer her? Weeks away from home. An occasional telephone call.

More secrets and more lies.

He crushed the cigarette butt in the ashtray on the table. Alex cursed the continued need for deception. No matter what, he had to return that journal. While he couldn't be completely honest with her, he could at least come clean about the journal.

Dammit! Why couldn't he be a regular guy who'd fallen for an incredible woman? He felt trapped and angry, but there wasn't much he could about it. Once he and Emelio wrapped up this case, he'd tell Meghan everything and pray she still wanted him.

ALEX ADMIRED the body-hugging fit of Meghan's long red silk dress as he watched her hips sway. She was finally wearing the red "seduce me" sandals. The shoes looked just as sexy as he'd imagined and they added an extra swing to her walk.

As they headed for Front Street, a balmy gust teased the flowing skirt, offering him a brief glimpse of her bare legs. He had to be in love if the sight of her ankles turned him on. He'd better start buying looser pants.

"You look beautiful tonight, Trouble."

"Thank you, Nick. I wish I could say the same, but you're wearing that green-and-gold nightmare shirt." She rolled her eyes dramatically while he laughed. "Where are we going anyway?"

"I promised you something special and it's almost time."

"Everything about the past three days has been special." She smiled at him, a look of tenderness in her eyes that added to his guilt.

Meghan's face lit up when they reached Mallory Square. A hundred or so people milled around the food carts, craftsmen and street buskers. Music drifted above the babble of vendors hawking their wares. Comedians and magicians showed off their talents while children chased each other over the cobbled terrace.

"Oh, Nick, this is some kind of festival!"

"Best of all, it happens every night."

She grabbed his arm and gave him an enchanting smile. "Every night? Really?"

Alex broke into a wide grin when he saw her childlike joy. "Welcome to the only city that makes a party out of the sunset. It's a tradition with the tourists as well as the locals."

The sun lit the sky with flaming red, bright orange and hot yellow. As it dropped beneath the horizon, the crowd roared in response. Caught up in the moment, Meghan screamed and cheered right along with them. When the last rays slid into the sea, she wrapped her arm about his waist.

"That was wonderful, Nick! What a great tradition. Thank you for sharing it with me."

He turned until she was in his embrace, quietly gazing into her eyes. The twilight both accentuated and hid the features of her face. Her dark hair was a mass of loose curls and she'd done that thing to her eyes again, making them look smoky and mysterious.

"I have to tell you something, Trouble. I didn't come to Cayo Sueño looking to meet anyone. In fact, it's the last thing I wanted."

She seemed to hold her breath, her whole body tense. He hesitated, wondering if it was too soon to declare his true feelings. Yeah, it was too soon. He needed to know for sure how she felt.

"Neither did I. My plan was just to have a sexual fling. I never expected…this."

Alex felt his heart stop, then stutter back to normal. *Let her say it. Please let her say it.* If she said it first, he could finally tell her the truth. "And what is 'this'?"

Meghan ducked her head, the hint of a smile on her lips. In the dim light, he thought he saw a blush steal over her cheeks. "I— I'm not sure yet. But I like it. I like you."

Okay. This is good. This is real good. But he couldn't voice the other words. Not yet. "I like you, too."

She crossed her arms, pretending to scowl. One eyebrow arched indignantly as she tilted her head to the side. "That's it?"

He flashed her a grin. "Okay. I like you *a lot.*"

"Nick!" Her voice rose in amused protest.

"Hey, it's more than you said."

"But I said it first. You have to do better."

He cocked his head, pretending to consider his answer. "Do you want to go steady?"

Meghan laughed and slid her arms up to his neck. "You make me crazy—"

Alex cupped her face in his palms and brushed his mouth over hers. He stared down at her, moved by a warm sense of rightness and belonging.

"I'm crazy about you, too."

"Where do we go from here?"

There was no way for him to know, not when he was supposed to be working the Ramos case instead of spending time with her. She was offering him all that he wanted, everything he needed. And damned if he could accept it with a clear conscience. Because none of it was real. She'd fallen for a man who was—and yet wasn't—him.

Where do we go from here? She meant their relationship, but he gave her the easy answer. "Let's eat."

Alex guided her to a two-story nineteenth-century Spanish colonial. A garden filled with bromeliads, sapodilla and palms surrounded the small hotel. Inside, a hostess showed them to a quiet table near the windows of the intimate restaurant.

Meghan looked around the elegant art deco dining room, approval obvious in her gaze. "I feel like we're at some chic little café on the Seine."

"The house was built in 1887, but the Hotel St. Pierre wasn't established until 1921. There're only twenty-seven rooms, no two exactly alike. This bistro serves contemporary cuisine, with a French influence."

"You must come here a lot."

"Nope. I read the brochure."

She laughed and picked up the menu. He admired her from across the table and discovered he had a voracious appetite. Only not for the food. The deep, lush red color on her lips ought to be illegal. Just looking at her mouth was getting him hard. After a moment, she looked up to catch him staring.

"What is it?"

"We could skip right to dessert." He leaned forward, his voice low and deep. "I have this urge to decorate your body with chocolate sauce and whipped cream, then lick it off."

A gleam of interest lit her eyes, but she rapped her menu against the table's edge. "Are you trying to starve me to death? We have yet to finish a whole meal together."

He shrugged good-naturedly. "A guy can dream."

"Well, dream on, Nick. I'm hungry."

"Me, too. Let me tell you about the banana and the nuts—"

"I know all about your banana, thank you." She winked at him in return.

A waiter brought over the appetizers and set them on the table. He opened a bottle of wine, poured and offered the sample to Alex. Meghan looked on, amused. They both knew he would have preferred a beer.

When she sipped her lobster bisque and moaned, the sound shot straight from his ears to his groin. Shifting a little in his seat, he watched her lick several drops of soup from her lower lip. He gulped his wine to clear the knot in his throat.

"This is wonderful. Try it." She held her spoon across the table to him.

Leaning forward, he slowly opened his mouth. He tasted the creamy soup laced with Spanish sherry, gazing at her intently while he did so. Her golden-brown eyes darkened with desire. "I never knew soup could be sexy. Do it again."

Chuckling, Alex speared a lump of crabmeat from his own plate, dipped it into the cilantro butter and offered it to her. "I'll eat yours if you eat mine."

She stuck out her tongue to take the delicate morsel from the fork into her mouth. "Not bad, I guess. For real crab cakes, you have to be in Maryland."

"Are you going to miss living there, now that you're going to school in Miami?"

"Not really. I've always hated the winters. If a single snowflake falls to the ground, everyone goes bananas."

"Speaking of bananas—"

"We were speaking of snowflakes."

Alex wiggled his eyebrows suggestively. "I forgot to tell you what I want to do with the caramel sauce and cherries."

"Tell me when I come back." She grinned before excusing herself to go to the ladies' room.

He stood when she left the table, noticing the looks of admiration Meghan got as she walked away.

There had to be a way for them to work things out. She'd be busy with school soon, anyway, so maybe his frequent absences wouldn't be a problem. Alex drummed his fingers on the table and idly glanced about the dining room.

A woman standing near the entrance caught his attention. When he recognized her, the wine turned to acid in his stomach. Adrenaline pumped though his system in a wave of ice, followed by a surge of heat. If Vivian was in town, Frankie Ramos couldn't be far behind.

Show time.

12

Light falls on the mirror and the face there changes. I look at myself and Elise stares back at me. As the evening shadows touch my reflection, I wonder if anyone is really who they seem....

MEGHAN STEPPED OUT of the ladies' room and into her worst nightmare. She forced a slow, angry breath between her cold lips. Some woman had wrapped her arms around Nick and was kissing him like a sailor come home from the sea.

Her eyes narrowed as she studied her competition. The woman seemed to believe "less is more" in terms of clothing and "more is better" in terms of makeup. She had the body of a Vegas showgirl under a gold sequined dress that clung to her generous bosom like plastic wrap.

Jealousy ate at her and, for a millisecond, she gave in to the idea of getting breast implants. Then reason returned. Nick liked her just the way she was.

In the past, she'd lost confidence in herself instead of realizing any man worth having would look for more in a woman than a pair of big breasts. That wasn't going to happen again. Meghan took a deep breath through flared nostrils and squared her shoulders.

No bimbo was going to compromise their budding relationship, not when they'd reached The Like Stage. She raised her chin and stalked over to the hostess desk, prepared for battle. "I think introductions are in order. Don't you?"

She noticed Nick's pupils dilate as he shifted uneasily away from the showgirl Velcroed to his side. "This is Vivian. She's…um… She's…"

She's a tramp with a capital T, finished Meghan. The woman was trailing her silver-tipped nails along Nick's arm and giving Meghan a canary feather-filled smile. It was really going to hurt when she started yanking every platinum hair off the bimbo's head.

"Oh, Alex and I go way back. Don't we?"

Alex? She called him Alex.

Meghan frowned in confusion. Was that some kind of pet name? His brows drew together and he gave Vivian a slight shake of his head. Obviously this woman knew him on a personal level if she had a nickname for him. The thought didn't make Meghan happy at all.

She stepped back to put some distance between them but Nick caught her arm. When she resisted, he slipped his hand around her waist, holding her close. "It's not what you think. Viv is a business acquaintance."

"You make it sound so impersonal." Vivian pouted before continuing in her annoying little-girl voice. "So, where have you been hiding? I haven't seen you since Lena's party."

"Yeah, well, I've been—" He glanced down at Meghan.

Vivian interrupted, pursing her lip in an expression

she'd obviously practiced many times. "Have you seen Rogelio?"

"No. I was looking for Braga earlier."

"He's supposed to be having dinner with us."

Nothing about Nick's appearance changed, but she sensed his agitation. Like a switch had been triggered, turning his energy level up a notch. "Who is 'us'?"

"Frankie should be here any minute now." As Vivian's voice lost its breathiness, Meghan suddenly recognized a spark of intelligence behind her blue eyes. "He didn't seem at all surprised that Rogelio hasn't been around today."

"Really?" Nick was deceptively nonchalant. "Braga was going to set up a meeting for me."

Vivian nodded. "I'll take care of it."

There was definitely something between them, but Meghan was no longer sure it was sexual.

"Thanks, Viv. I appreciate that."

"Try showing it sometime. You know where I live."

Okay. Maybe it was sexual after all. Meghan glared at both of them and leaned into Nick, guarding her territory.

He squeezed her hip in reassurance, refusing the bait Vivian dangled. "We've got to go. Our food is getting cold."

"Me, too. My table is ready. Good seeing you, Alex. Give me a call when you get back to Miami." She blew a little kiss toward his mouth before she walked away.

Meghan stepped aside and planted a hand on her hip. "All right. I want to know—"

"Not now."

Nick abruptly caught her by the elbow and she

gasped. He didn't hurt her, but his grip was firm as he steered her into the dining room. She tolerated it until they got back to the table, then shook off his hand. She took her seat, clenching both fists in her lap.

I won't cause a scene. I may seriously hurt him, but I won't make a scene.

Meghan gulped half of her wine in one swallow, not caring if she got drunk again. She glanced up to see Vivian watching her from across the restaurant, a sly grin on her heavily made-up face. With a determined set to her shoulders, she set the glass back on the table. No way would she let that tramp see her lose control. Whatever was going on, she'd deal with it head-on.

"Start talking, *Alex*. And I suggest you talk fast."

He faced her silently, reluctance casting a shadow over his face. Displeasure turned his eyes from light green to jade. Looking at the mask his features had taken on frightened her. It also made her mad.

"Just who is that woman to you?"

"An exotic dancer and paid escort."

She snorted in disgust. "So Vivian is the type of beer-drinking, uncomplicated blonde you prefer?"

"Viv introduced me to Rogelio Braga last year. He's my connection to the Ramos cartel."

What was going on? A chill shuddered along her spine, then spread over her whole body. "Who the hell are you?"

His eyes widened in surprise.

Unbelievable. He knew her well enough to notice one out-of-character swearword. Meanwhile, she'd had no clue he was some low-life drug dealer. "Answer my question."

Nick leaned forward so she could hear him over the

din of conversation without raising his voice. "You've got to promise not to repeat anything I tell you."

Meghan tilted her head to the side and arched one brow. "We have an agreement. No promises, remember?"

"This is serious—"

"Then stop stalling. Who are you?"

He pinched the bridge of his nose, briefly closing his eyes. "I shouldn't trust you, but you're right. I do owe you some kind of answers."

He might as well have stabbed her with his steak knife. He shouldn't trust her? The irony of this bordered on the absurd. She gazed at the mouth that had kissed her, the arms that had held her, the body that had loved her.

"You certainly trusted me in bed."

"It's nothing personal."

Some sound of distress must have escaped because he jerked his head up. "No, wait, I didn't mean it like that. Making love with you was personal. It's the other part—"

She raised one palm to stop his words. "I'm waiting for an explanation, Nick. Or is it Alex? What am I supposed to call you?"

"My name is Alex Worth. Nicholas Alexander Worth."

"Why did you tell me your name was Nick Alexander?"

He slowly exhaled, seeming to have trouble meeting her eye. He was probably trying to come up with a good story.

"I'm an agent with the Department of Justice...."

She decided she was having a stroke. Her heart

seized and her whole body went numb, and the blood pounding in her ears drowned out the rest of his words.

Nick was a cop. Just like Kyle.

"I work for the DEA out of the Miami field office. Rogelio Braga isn't really my client—he's a money launderer. I've been after his boss in the cartel for two years."

She saw his mouth moving, but didn't hear anything else he said. Well, at least he wasn't a low-life drug dealer. Just a danger junkie with a badge. Interlacing her fingers on the table to keep them from trembling, she continued to stare.

"You're a secret agent who's been lying to me since the day we met. You were going to keep lying to me until—until when exactly?" Meghan waved one hand vaguely in the air.

He averted his gaze and rubbed the scar on his temple. His mouth was tight, his expression grim. When he looked up, her own turbulent emotions were reflected in the kaleidoscope of his eyes.

"You were never going to tell me."

"I've been in the Justice Department long enough to know better than to jeopardize an ongoing investigation." He leaned forward and caught her wrist. "I'm doing it anyway."

Trying to pull her arm away, she looked at him in confusion. "*I'm* under investigation?"

"No. I was suspicious of you at first—"

"Of me? Why?"

"I had reason to think you were involved with Braga, especially when I saw you two together." That explained his strange behavior in the lounge the first night and on the pier the next day. He loosened his grip and she succeeded in twisting out of his grasp.

A truly ugly thought occurred to her. Bitterness churned in her stomach and she fought hard to control it. "At what point, *exactly,* did you decide that I was above suspicion?"

His eyes were bleak and his voice sounded resigned. The corners of his mouth turned down. "I cleared you when I got the results of a background check."

"You told someone to poke around in my life? You had somebody dig into my past?"

Nick reached for her hand again, but she snatched it away. "I had to. I had to know who you were."

And all the while, *he* knew who he *wasn't.* How ironic that they'd both been pretending to be someone else. Her throat was tight, choked with unshed tears. He still hadn't answered the question burning a hole in her gut. She crossed her arms, gripping her elbows hard enough to leave bruises.

"Did you take me to bed before, or after, you found out?"

He dropped his head, eyes closed briefly, and cursed softly under his breath. Then he looked at her, his voice filled with conviction. "After. I swear it was after."

"Do you have any idea how this makes me feel?" She spoke in a broken whisper, not fully believing him.

"When I thought you were working for Braga, I couldn't tell you about my assignment. Then, when I knew you weren't involved, I kept quiet to protect you."

She toyed with her wineglass, twirling the stem between her fingers. Her anger gradually abated, leaving a strangely hollow feeling of disappointment. Despite her intentions, she'd fallen deeply in love with Nick...*Alex*...only to discover he was the last type of man she wanted to get involved with. A layer of ice stole over her heart, the heart she'd so recently and freely given to a man she didn't know.

"I never meant to hurt you, Meghan. And I'm sorry about this, about getting you mixed up in my case."

She sighed, twirling her glass in the other direction. "Why tell me now, all of a sudden? You could have pretended Vivian was an old girlfriend."

"I don't have a choice. A few months ago, the DEA raided one of Francisco Ramos's warehouses. We got word that a large drug shipment was coming in."

"And?"

"One of the informants turned out to be double-crossing us. As a result, my partner's cover was blown and I got this." He pointed to his scar.

She frowned as something clicked in her memory. "That was in Overtown, wasn't it? The story of the arrests was all over the news. If I remember correctly, two people were killed in the shooting."

His gaze suddenly focused over her shoulder. She was perversely fascinated to watch the change come over him. His lips flattened into a cynical smile as he set his jaw, the warmth faded from his eyes and his features hardened. Suddenly his face looked...different.

"There's one more thing I need to tell you."

His cold, ruthless tone unnerved her. It was the same voice she'd heard during his nightmare. "I don't think I want to know anything else."

"The 'Frankie' Vivian referred to, the one she's meeting for dinner, is Francisco Ramos." He dipped his chin to indicate there was someone behind her. "That's Frankie. And he's headed this way."

"What? He's coming over right now?"

Meghan stared in horror, praying he'd made a mistake. She drew a shallow, unhappy breath when he remained silent. Cautiously angling her head to one side, she peered out of the corner of her eyes.

An attractive Latino man walked purposefully toward them. He had the lean, compact build of a prizefighter under his pastel blue T-shirt and linen blazer. Ramos had the look of someone who demanded instant obedience—and got it.

Icy panic swept over her, draining the blood from her face. Turning back around, she spoke in a quavering whisper. "What are we going to do?"

"Calm down and listen to me. *Listen, Meghan.* If we simply play it cool, we'll get through this."

His voice was low and soothing but the mask he still wore did nothing to reassure her. Reaching across the table, he took her trembling fingers in his. She couldn't tell which of their palms was sweating and yet he looked amazingly relaxed and confident.

She wondered if he was always this good an actor. Each and every moment of their time together was now questionable. She pushed the doubts aside to be dealt with later. Right now her heart was pounding in her chest and she felt light-headed. "I think we should leave—"

"History is *not* going to repeat itself tonight, for either of us. Just trust me and I'll get you out of here as quickly as possible."

"This is hardly the time to talk about trust."

"Good, you've got your spirit back." He squeezed

her fingers gently, then released her hand and sat back in his chair. "Now smile, Trouble, but stay quiet. Remember, my name is Nicholas Alexander and I'm an investment broker."

He shifted his gaze behind her and rose to his feet in one smooth motion. Meghan could only stare as he changed yet again. Now his expression was eager, his attitude obsequious as Ramos approached their table.

"Señor Ramos. Thank you for inviting me to Cayo Sueño."

Ramos ignored "Nick's" outstretched hand, his mouth drawn into a semblance of greeting. "Rogelio made those arrangements, not I."

"Nevertheless, I look forward to discussing your financial needs. I have several ideas—"

"I have some ideas of my own. Most of them revolve around the last time we met."

Nick dropped his arm to his side and held Ramos's gaze. "That was a very unfortunate incident."

His tone was still courteous but somehow insolent as well. Ramos's lips thinned and his smile grew brittle. Meghan wasn't the only one who noticed the undertone. Was this animosity supposed to be the broker's or did it come from the agent? Her pulse fluttered as a wave of apprehension swept over her.

"The wound on your forehead seems to have healed nicely. It makes an interesting souvenir, does it not?"

"That night was more fortunate for some than for others. *You* were able to avoid any mementos."

"I've often thought of you since then. It has occurred to me that perhaps you were responsible, either by stupidity or by intent." Ramos obviously suspected "Nick Alexander" wasn't who he appeared to be.

"Why would I jeopardize what I hope will be a profitable relationship for both of us?" Nick sat down and reached for the wine bottle. He took his time refilling the glasses. "Vivian tells me Señor Braga is…unavailable. Either by stupidity or by intent."

"What do you mean?"

"Just the other day, he and I were discussing some possible changes in your organization." He casually draped one arm along the back of his chair. "In fact he said, and I quote, that he would 'take care of it personally.'"

Ramos's black eyes went flat and lifeless in response to the taunt. "I should have taken better aim."

He was the one who shot Nick? Meghan's gaze flew to his face and she watched him master his reaction. He didn't move a muscle and the very stillness gave him away. His expression didn't change as, using his middle finger, he stroked the scar over his eyebrow.

"Accidents happen."

While the two men continued their verbal sparring, she twisted the napkin around her fingers. Everything would be fine. "Nick" could look after himself. In fact, the more she considered it, the more she realized that he could handle any situation that came up. Look how well he'd handled her.

But what if she was wrong?

What if Ramos discovered his organization had been infiltrated? What would happen then? Could anyone identify Nick or find out where he lived? Omigod, what if they hurt or even killed him? Meghan shivered and glanced over at Ramos, upset by the direction her thoughts had taken.

His smile was as fake as Vivian's cleavage. "It

seems I may have misjudged you, Nick. Why don't you join me for a drink? We can discuss your ideas for my investments.''

"I'd like that very much. I definitely have some plans for you. But, as you can see, I have a prior commitment.''

Ramos suddenly turned his head, as if noticing her for the first time. He ogled her like an éntree on the menu. Inwardly, Meghan shrank from the unwanted attention.

"And who is your lovely companion?''

"She's a friend.'' Nick spoke sharply, too sharply, drawing Ramos's attention. "I'd be happy to meet with you any time tomorrow. When would it be convenient?''

Ramos just stared while he rattled off some possible times. Displeasure showed in his expression.

Meghan made a decision. *I can do this. I know I can.* As soon as the thought entered her mind, a sense of calm washed over her. The last time she'd been in a dangerous situation, her panic had made it worse. She couldn't face that kind of guilt and remorse again. This time she'd make sure the circumstances turned in her favor. The only way to protect Nick's identity was to maintain his cover.

She was about to step in way over her head, but echoes from the past were calling her to action. So were visions of the future, one she wanted to share with the man who'd shown her how to be the woman in her fantasies. She thought about her diary. On those pages, she was bold, daring, sexy and in control. Well, here was an opportunity to live the adventure. Excitement accelerated her pulse.

One really bad girl, coming up.

Ramos was ogling her again. "I am still waiting for you to introduce your friend."

"She's nobody."

"Nobody?" She plastered on an arrogant smile. Arching one brow, she tilted her head. "You're a naughty boy, *Nicky*. I'll have to punish you later."

Confusion darted across his face. She held his gaze, silently begging him to go along with her charade. His pupils dilated and his mouth tightened in disapproval when he realized what she was doing.

She turned to Ramos, her gaze sliding over him insolently. Trying for a jaded expression, she regally extended one hand toward him. She was confident, she was daring and she had attitude to spare.

Ramos leaned over her hand as if to kiss it. "And what is your name, my dear?"

"Elise Foster. I'm his mistress."

13

For so long, too long, I've been living a lie. I want to be someone else....

ALEX HAD NO IDEA what the hell kind of fantasy Meghan was acting out, but she'd chosen the wrong audience. He inhaled slowly, forcing air past the pressure in his chest.

Ramos was obviously intrigued—her hand was still caught in his grasp and his black eyes took on a reptilian quality. "His mistress, eh? How very bold of you to admit it."

"In my business, I have to be bold." "Elise" slipped her fingers away, regarding him with the look of a woman who'd long ago set a price on her appeal.

Alex clenched the muscles along his torso to keep himself from shaking. She was trying to take part in a world even he had difficulty handling right now. And he couldn't stop her.

Ramos continued to assess her. "Which business is that, Miss—?"

"Mistress. With a capital *M*. I'm helping Nicky with a...discipline problem." Her sly look left no question what kind of discipline was being meted out. Ramos laughed.

Caught off guard, Alex's mind instantly produced an image of "Elise" wearing the studded leather outfit they'd seen earlier. Judging by the expression on Ramos's face, his thoughts had gone in the same direction.

Wait until I get you alone, Trouble. After this little stunt, she'd be the one with the discipline problem. Meantime, he had to get back in the game. "So, about your capital investments, Señor Ramos…"

Ramos ignored him. His gaze wandered over Meghan's body in a way that made Alex want to tear him apart, piece by slimy piece. "I am staying in one of the suites upstairs, Elise. Perhaps we can—"

"No." He spit the word out in a cold, uncompromising tone. The scar on his temple throbbed viciously. No way would he let her go anywhere with that crazy bastard.

"Elise" shook her head emphatically. "I don't do threesomes. Not without forty-eight hours notice and payment up front."

Alex coughed to hide a surprised chuckle. Lord, what a woman. He was actually impressed by her bored expression and been-there-done-him attitude. If he wasn't so damned mad, he might have admired the skill with which she pulled off the con.

Ramos flicked a dismissive glance in his direction. "My offer did not include Mr. Alexander. Surely his little problem will not require much of your time."

Alex snickered at the veiled insult to his manhood. Meghan kicked his shin under the table before he could retort, then spoke in a dismissive tone.

"I'll check my schedule and give you a call, Frankie."

Ramos leaned down to whisper something in her ear. Alex was too far away to hear what he said and too close not to notice Frankie's gaze drop down to her cleavage.

With a condescending look, her lips twisted into an amused smirk. "I get that request a lot, though not usually from men of your reputation."

Ramos's eyes narrowed and he straightened abruptly. "What has Mr. Alexander told you about me?"

"We've been way too busy to talk about you, Frankie." She took a sip of her wine, then licked the residue from her mouth. "Besides, I'm sure everything I've heard is true."

This time, Alex tapped her shin under the table, silently warning her to back off.

Ramos inclined his head, acknowledging the barb. Then he indicated the corner table where he'd left Vivian. "I seem to be neglecting my dinner companion. Won't you join us for dessert?"

Meghan looked across the table, her whiskey-colored eyes gleaming with excitement. She reached up, index finger extended, to stroke her lower lip suggestively. "We already made plans for dessert, didn't we, lover?"

The intimate gesture had an immediate effect on Alex. His pulse was racing for a different reason now. But, her plans had to wait until after a long lecture about the danger she'd put herself in. "We'll have to pass this time, Señor Ramos. But I'd still like to meet tomorrow."

Ramos kept his gaze focused on Meghan. "I have

arranged a gathering in the resort casino for Friday night. It would please me to have you there, Elise.''

''I'm sure it will be quite entertaining.'' She dipped her head imperiously, as if the invitation was expected and no less than she deserved. ''We'll be there, won't we, Nicky.''

It was more of a statement than a question. Alex hid his amusement behind a bland expression. ''Your command is my wish, Mistress.''

Ramos sneered at him with contempt. ''A real man wouldn't reveal his weakness so.''

''Elise'' laughed, a husky peal of genuine delight. ''Nicky is a real man. He's definitely held my interest these past few days. And I'm not even charging him.''

Now she was starting to play it over the top. He needed to take control of the situation, but he had to admit he was fascinated. Ramos wasn't paying him a damned bit of attention anyway—

Alex narrowed his eyes as Ramos trailed his fingers covetously along Meghan's arm. Then he laid his hand on her bare shoulder. ''You have not been with a real man until you've been with me.''

Her gaze pierced him like shards of jagged glass. Her tone was equally cutting. ''I didn't give you permission to touch me. If we make a business arrangement, you had better be able to follow instructions.''

Holy shit.

Alex felt the air around him begin to sizzle. The expression on Ramos's face had him flexing his fists. Given the drug kingpin's reputation for erratic behavior, he wasn't sure what to expect. Fear twisted itself around his heart, stabbing vicious fingers into his belly.

"Elise" was going to get them both killed with that mouth of hers.

Just then Meghan looked over at him and very subtly winked. Alex stared at her in amazement before hiding his reaction. She was actually enjoying this! Part of him wanted to kiss her senseless, while the other part wanted to shake some common sense into her.

Ramos removed his hand and flushed, but his eyes gleamed with sexual excitement. "I'll look forward to Friday, then."

Alex waited until they were alone, until his heart rate slowed and his temper faded. It would take a lot longer to get his conflicting emotions under control. Finally he spoke from between clenched teeth. "Have you lost your mind?"

Meghan tossed her head and grinned triumphantly. "I did a good job and you know it."

"You weren't supposed to do anything but sit there and *you* know it." He gulped the last of his wine then set the glass down with a thump. "Let's go, Trouble."

MEGHAN KICKED OFF HER SHOES and began pacing the living room, too agitated to even write in her diary. She had no idea what had possessed her, but it felt *good!* She was flying high with no intention of coming down.

The adrenaline rushing through her system had to be better than any drug. It also made her horny. Nick had told her to wait while he checked in with his office. She couldn't wait much longer. He was going to get pounced the second he stepped over the threshold.

Where is he, where is he, where is he?

When she strode back over to the picture window,

she caught sight of herself in the dark glass. The color on her cheeks was high, her pupils were dilated and her nipples had beaded against the material of her dress. *Omigod. I'm burning up. Where is he?*

At the sharp knock, she dashed across the suite and swung the door wide. Nick barely glanced at her before he swept past and headed for the living room. Still, she was able to gauge his mood from her brief look at his expression. His face was alive with emotions ranging from irritation to lust.

She'd just concentrate on the lust part.

Meghan stalked toward him, growling deep in her throat. He turned at the sound and she leaped into his embrace. Wrapping her arms about his neck, she kissed him with a hunger both demanding and desperate. She arched her body against his, aflame with primal need.

"We need to talk."

"Later."

"Now. That was some performance you gave tonight. You had me half believing you really are a dominatrix."

She laughed, tilting her head invitingly. "Get out your handcuffs and I'll make you believe it completely."

Meghan ravaged his mouth while her hands slid over his back and down to fumble with his belt buckle. He kissed her back and she felt the hard evidence of his passion against her belly. Then he set her back on her feet with an audible sigh.

She wiggled her hips against his zipper. "Let's get crazy naked, baby. I need you bad."

For a second, desire flared in his green eyes but then

he shook his head. Releasing her, Nick took a step back and frowned. "We really have to talk."

"Urrgh! Now?"

"You took one hell of a chance tonight, Trouble. I could have sworn I told you to stay quiet."

Okay. Lust would have to wait a few minutes. Too restless to stand still, she started pacing the room again. She was breathless with exhilaration over the memory. "I was going to, I swear. But then I just sort of got into the role. And it worked! Ramos bought it. He bought every single word."

"Well, he won't be buying you, 'Mistress Elise.' Your days of undercover work are over." His voice was heavy with sarcasm.

"But, Nick, I got us invited to the casino Friday night. You're closer to Ramos now than you would have been without me!"

He abruptly caught her elbow when she flitted past him. "Look, I'll admit your persona complemented my cover. And don't think I'm not grateful for your help. But you put both of us at risk. You gambled—"

"And I won! That's what it's all about, isn't it? Matching wits with an adversary and coming out on top." She grinned up at him, delighted by her accomplishment. "That's the appeal, that's the fun. Because you can't be sure, really sure, you pulled it off. This is such a rush!"

"This is adrenaline talking, not the woman who said cops were as bad as gigolos and perverts." Nick dropped her arm and took off his sports jacket, then tossed it at the armchair.

Her smile faded, her mood plummeting as his words sank in. Kyle. How could she have forgotten? She'd sworn she wanted nothing to do with law enforcement, and yet she'd gotten off on playing Secret Agent Girl. What had she been thinking? She could have ruined everything for his case against Ramos and Braga.

"Believe me, honey, I know what you're feeling. There's nothing like the combination of fear and thrill pumping through your veins. I've been addicted to it for years…until now." He collapsed onto the sofa, resting one ankle over the opposite knee.

"I guess—" She folded her arms across her waist and ducked her head. "I guess I got caught up in the moment, in the chance to be someone else."

"It isn't as fun and glamorous as you seem to think. Agents work long hours in dangerous surroundings. All for little pay and even less appreciation."

"And there's a lot of risk involved." Meghan sighed, a deep unhappiness settling in her chest. Nick was a cop, a man who took risks, chased danger and who one night wouldn't come home.

"You take the chances when you take the badge." He sounded tired, disgruntled, as he raked a hand through his hair.

She laughed humorlessly. "Kyle used to say, 'This is my job. I protect and I serve.' The worst part is he believed it."

"A lot of us do, Meghan. That's how we sleep at night and still dive back into the filth the next morning."

"Then why do it? Why do you keep doing it?"

His expression grew still and his gaze seemed to turn inward. "Any sacrifice is worth it if someone gets one more day with their husband, their daughter…or their brother."

She picked up on the underlying sadness immediately. Sitting down next to him, she took his hand. "Tell me about *your* brother. Tell me about Greg."

Alex turned his hand until their palms met. He stared down at the carpet, haunted by memories. With each image flashing across his mind, the band of pain tightened around his chest, making it hard to draw breath.

If he was truly going to be honest with Meghan, he'd have to bare his soul and let her see into the place where old grief and raw guilt lived. Maybe if she understood about his brother, she'd understand what drove him.

"Greg got into drugs in high school. The heroin made him crazy, reckless, thoughtless. He didn't care about anything except his next fix. My parents were beside themselves, having to watch their youngest son destroy himself."

"What happened?"

Alex cleared his throat. He never talked about this with anyone, not even his parents. He scrubbed his face impatiently with his palms. "I let him down, that's what happened. I was going to college, couldn't look after him like I should have. Greg dropped out of school, disappearing for weeks at a time."

"So where is he now?"

"No idea. The last time I saw him was after he got arrested on possession charges. He looked like a corpse. Thin and dirty and strung out. The judge ordered rehab, but Greg walked away after only two weeks. He kept walking."

Sliding her arm around his waist, Meghan leaned her head on his shoulder. Alex closed his eyes for a moment, accepting the comfort. "I tried to talk to him, tried to help him, but he'd become a stranger. Truth is, I lost my kid brother long before he vanished.''

"And so you joined the DEA, looking for revenge."

He opened his eyes and glanced down at her. As usual, his career came between them. "I'm sorry for checking your background, but—"

She touched her fingers to his lips and shook her head. "There's nothing we need to discuss. I understand you have a job to do."

"A job that could affect our relationship. It already has."

Meghan got up from the sofa. He felt her withdraw from him emotionally as well as physically. When she finally looked over at him, her gaze was remote. "Do we have a relationship? This was supposed to be strictly physical, remember."

Alex stared at her, disappointed, until she glanced away. He thought they'd grown closer over the last couple of days, but here she was putting up barriers again. "Yeah, I forgot. No strings, no promises and no regrets."

She had the grace to blush as bitterness seeped into his tone. He continued to stare, frustrated by pent-up emotions she only let him express in bed. He was good enough to give her body to, but not her heart. He could be a fantasy lover, but not her love.

My fantasy lover stands beside me under the waterfall. He moves toward me, offers himself to me. Our bodies join beneath the cascade....

Alex stood up and pulled his shirt over his head without bothering with the buttons. Meghan watched him undress with a guarded look on her face. When he hauled her roughly into his arms, she put a hand on his chest as if to stop him. She must have recognized the heat in his gaze for the anger it really was.

Reaching behind her, he unzipped her dress and peeled it from her body. He slipped his hand inside of her panties, felt the slick dampness between her legs. Then he stepped back to take off his pants and the bright green silk boxers she'd bought.

He took her hand and led her toward the bathroom. After grabbing a couple condoms, he reached into the shower and opened the faucet. His hands encircled her waist, lifting her onto the vanity, while the water heated. He kissed her slowly, thoroughly, wanting to show her what was missing from their arrangement, trying to ease the empty feeling inside. Damn her rules!

Meghan moaned while he caressed and fondled the soft weight of her breasts. She placed both hands on either side of his face and deepened the kiss, exploring his mouth with her tongue. Then she wrapped her legs around his thighs, pulling him closer. Dampness formed where his penis made contact with her womanly flesh.

A raging need built inside him as the bathroom filled with steam. He quickly rolled the condom on before guiding her under the spray and closing the shower door. Rivulets of hot water trailed over his shoulders and down his chest. Meghan stuck out her tongue to catch the water dripping off one nipple. When she took the hardened peak into her hot mouth, he cupped the back of her neck and pulled her up to claim her mouth once more.

She reached for the tropical-fruit-scented shower gel and poured some into her palms. After working up a lather on his skin, she used her body to wash them both by rubbing against him. Then she put her hands to better use. She took him between her fingers and slid her gel-covered palm along his shaft.

Her touch was sweet torment as she gently squeezed and fondled him. Alex growled deep in his throat, fighting for control. If he didn't hold back, he'd come in her hand. But he couldn't wait any longer. He had to have her now.

She gasped as he pushed her up against the shower door. Pressing his body to hers, he rubbed one thigh between hers, stroking her. She tilted her head, eyes closed in pleasure. He slipped his hands along her wet skin and ducked his head to nibble the sensitive base of her neck. Her whimpers of longing echoed his own need. Now, dammit. Right now.

He turned her until she leaned her palms against the tiled wall. The shower cascaded through her hair, down her back and over her thighs. He moved his hands to her waist, pulled her hips back and took her from behind. It was a raw act of possession. Meghan grabbed the towel rack with one hand for support as her knees buckled. With her other hand still splayed against the wall, she arched her back to meet him.

He nudged her legs apart, widening her stance. Then he continued to thrust into her, pushing deeper, burying himself to the hilt. Alex felt the change inside her, felt her tighten around him. The sensation was almost more than he could stand.

Closing his eyes, he was acutely aware of the smell of sex and pineapple. The sounds of the spray hitting the tiles and of their lust echoing in the small room. The slick feeling of the water on his skin and his slick flesh inside of her.

He barely managed to hold off his own climax as her body enveloped him in the heat and pressure of her orgasm. She cried out as her body trembled around him. Only his strength kept her from slipping to the tile floor, and only sheer determination kept him from coming inside her. Before she could even catch her breath, he turned off the shower faucet and opened the door.

Lifting her into his arms, he carried her, dripping wet, into the bedroom. The sex was great, but damned if he was going to settle for that. He needed her to want more from him. They'd had sex; now they were going to make love. He was going to teach her the difference between a fantasy and a dream come true.

After laying her down on the bed, he draped his body over hers as she opened her arms. He claimed her mouth while her fingers tangled in his hair. Overwhelmed by the intensity of his feelings, he took his time despite the fierce need to get inside her again.

He was lucky to have her. He knew Meghan in ways she didn't know herself. He'd come to value her strengths, and accept her insecurities. She was a beautiful and caring woman. She was smart and funny and passionate. And she was going to be his.

When she parted her thighs, he pushed into her wet passage, inch by inch, drawing out the moment of joining. He eased back and then slowly squeezed forward again, shuddering with the fulfillment of it. She arched toward him when he sank into her, their bodies becoming one. Lifting his head to see her face, Alex watched her as he claimed her as his own.

"I love you, Meghan."

The words rushed out in a hoarse whisper. Her eyes

widened in surprise before she squeezed them shut, blocking him out. He rocked his hips forward, increasing the friction along with the pace. Her hands stroked his back, urging him on. She wiggled and strained beneath him. He began thrusting heavily, needing release, needing her reaction.

"I love you," he repeated.

He'd never felt so scared, so damn vulnerable. His breath hitched and his heart thudded in his chest as he waited for her response. The emotions shifting across her face mirrored the strong feelings twisting him up inside.

She looked fragile, achingly beautiful. A trembling smile touched her mouth. When she opened her eyes, tears fell from her lashes. Her quick intake of breath was part sigh and part sob.

"I love you, too, Nick."

His eyes filled while she held his gaze. She'd finally said the words he so desperately wanted to hear, but she'd said them to the wrong man. The weight of his emotions threatened to crush him but it was too late to stop.

He plunged into her, feeling her quiver with each powerful thrust. The pressure built as she kissed him wildly, lifting her body to meet his. He moved inside her, fast and hard. When he felt her go over the edge, he finally allowed himself to follow.

Hours later, Alex was still awake. With a sigh, he stared down at Meghan's sleeping form. Gently, cautiously, so he didn't wake her, he reached out to touch her face. When he caressed her cheek, she snuggled against his palm. His heart stuttered and bled.

She'd called him Nick, dammit.

He wanted her to love *him,* not the fantasy she'd created, not the man he pretended to be. He was trapped in a hell of his own making. Earlier tonight he'd asked her to trust him, knowing he wasn't worthy of it. And now he had to do something that would further test whatever might exist between them. He had to return her journal. If he didn't do it now he'd never gain her trust. And their future depended on that.

HE LOVED HER!

Meghan stretched lazily, a smile on her lips. What an incredible night. Danger made a great aphrodisiac. She rolled over, reaching out as she turned. The bed sheet felt cool and she opened her eyes to find Nick had already gotten up. Still, she felt his presence in the soreness of her body, the elation in her heart.

And yet in the back of her mind, she realized it couldn't last. Now that she knew he worked undercover, a much more dangerous job than Kyle's, her rules had to stay in place. She sighed and tossed the covers aside. She didn't want to deal with this now. They still had three days together. She wasn't going to waste them on "what if."

She swung her legs over the edge of the bed and got up. Then she stretched again, enjoying the feel of the morning breeze on her naked body. In the living room, she grabbed a cola out of the minibar. Ahh, caffeine. After a few more gulps to get her brain working, she turned to see Nick out on the balcony.

Barefoot and bare-chested, he leaned his elbows on the rail, smoking a cigarette. Sunlight and shadows played over the muscles of his back and shoulders. His trousers stretched tight over his rear, accentuating his strong thighs. Meghan swallowed another mouthful of soda, admiring the view.

"Good morning, love. It's a beautiful day, isn't it?"

He turned immediately at the sound of her voice, but his smile didn't reach his eyes. Maybe he was worried about the case against Ramos. After tamping out his cigarette, he came back inside. "Morning. Did you sleep okay?"

"Like a rock. When the adrenaline finally drained out of my system, I just crashed."

Wanting to kiss him, she reached up to cup his cheek. Then she noticed his distant expression. Something other than the case was upsetting him. Studying his face, her arm fell to her side. "What's wrong, Nick?"

"My name is Alex." His voice was soft, but held an edge.

"I'm sorry, Alex. It's hard to get used to."

Sadness darkened his eyes before he glanced away, stuffing his fists into his pockets. "We should probably talk about last night."

Her bright mood slowly faded in the wake of her growing disquiet. What in the world was bothering him? "Last night was...incredible."

"Not exactly a waterfall, but I think it was a pretty good substitute." He spoke quietly and his eyes clouded with regret.

"Waterfall?" Momentarily confused, her brows drew together in a frown. The word hung in the air as a shiver of apprehension danced along her spine. "What are you—?"

She gasped, eyes wide. Her body stiffened with

shock and her pulse tripped into overdrive. Was he referring to—? No. He couldn't be… One look at his face confirmed her suspicion.

Oh. My. God!

14

He is the perfect lover. At times, patiently tender;
other times, fiercely passionate. He brings to life
my reckless longings, my deepest secrets, my
wildest desires.

WHITE-HOT FURY ENGULFED HER and she slammed the
can down, splashing cola all over the table. In that instant, she was very aware of her nudity. Knowing
Nick—Alex had violated her privacy made her feel exposed, humiliated.

Meghan snatched the dress she'd worn last night off
the floor. Her hands fisted as she quickly wrapped it to
shield her body. They remained clenched between her
breasts while his deceit ripped open her heart.

"You read my diary, didn't you? You've had it all
along!"

"Darling—"

"Don't."

She snapped out the command as she stalked back
to the bedroom. Mortified and resentful, she grabbed
her bathrobe off the dresser. The sound of muttered
expletives reached her ears as she tied the belt around
her waist.

He appeared in the doorway, raking several strands

of dark hair from his forehead. Then he held out her diary in his left hand. "I'm really sorry, Meghan. I never meant for you to find out."

"Is that supposed to be an apology?"

She angrily snatched the book from his grasp and clutched it against her chest. Diary pages flashed across her memory, intimate words that represented her hopes and dreams and fantasies. He'd read those words. All of them. *No one* knew as much about her as Nick— *Alex* now did.

"Do you make a habit of prying into the personal lives of strangers?" She shook her head. "Never mind." It was a stupid question, considering what he did for a living. She felt so pathetic. Practically begging him to be her lover, she'd made it easy for him to take advantage of her.

"Give me a break, Meghan. You left it out in plain view. Anyone would have been curious, especially after seeing the underwear in your luggage."

"Okay. That might explain why you skimmed through it. But you *kept* it and then *lied* to me when I asked if you'd seen it!" She shoved past him and went out into the living room. Still clutching the diary in one arm, she snatched up his clothes and flung them at him. "Get dressed and go."

Alex caught his shirt but the socks landed back on the floor. He started to put it on, then cursed. He undid the buttons before shoving his arms through the sleeves. "I'm not leaving. I need you to understand and to accept my apology."

Meghan stared like she'd never seen him before and slumped onto the sofa. The robe fell open and his gaze to her bare calves. Noticing his glance, she snapped the material over her legs. When he looked back at her face, she eyed him stonily.

"You had no right to read through my diary. How could you do such a despicable thing? Some things are meant to remain fantasies."

"And some things are meant to be real. You asked me to make your dreams come true, remember?"

Meghan scowled at him in disbelief. Blood pounded in her temples, further heating her face. This guy was truly unbelievable. "You crossed the line, Alex. And then, to add insult to injury, you used what you read to manipulate me."

She held the diary out accusingly. "That afternoon on the beach, the romantic dinner of my favorite foods and last night in the shower? You didn't seduce me— I seduced myself. Whatever intimacy I felt when we made love was as superficial as your personality."

He dropped into the armchair with a ragged sigh. Strain tightened the skin around his eyes. "It was never my intention to manipulate you. I wanted to be your fantasy lover. I wanted to make your dreams come true."

"Well, you did. You played the role exactly as I'd written it." She spat the words out, her voice rife with contempt.

Meghan jerked to her feet and went out on the balcony. Gulping in drafts of fresh air, she gripped the railing and tried to control the fine tremors in her hands. Alex came out a moment later, still barefoot, tucking his shirt into his trousers.

"I'm sorry for violating your privacy. But I'm not sorry I got the chance to discover who you really are."

She scoffed bitterly, squinting over her shoulder at

him. "Be sure and let me know when you figure out who *you* are."

Alex rested his shoulder on the door frame, wisely keeping his distance. "I'm the same guy you fell in love with. The one who fell in love with you."

Meghan shook her head. The fact that he'd hidden parts of himself—his identity, his job and his true purpose—made him seem like a stranger. Once again, she'd taken a man at his word, trusted him at face value. How dumb could one woman be?

"You're not the person I thought you were. *I'm* not even the person I thought I was." She looked down at the slim volume in her hand. When she finally turned in his direction, she couldn't see him through the veil of unshed tears.

"I've always been the good girl, always done the right thing. When I came to Cayo Sueño, my insecurity goaded me into being someone I'm not. The price I'm paying for that mistake is higher than I ever expected."

He came across the balcony in two long strides, his eyes intense. He gently pinched her chin between his thumb and index finger, willing her to look at him. His gaze burned into hers as he spoke with quiet conviction. "The woman I discovered inside these pages is sensual and passionate and comfortable with her sexuality. It's obvious you wanted to let that woman live outside your journal. I didn't mean to hurt you, Meghan. I wanted to make you happy—"

"Gee, thanks. Telling me that you love me was a nice touch, by the way. Which page did you steal that from?"

"I *do* love you. Being with you is extraordinary. And it's real, every moment, every touch…"

Hearing his words, but no longer believing them, tears slid down her cheeks.

His rough voice continued to seduce her. "It was special for me. You're special to me. What we have—"

"Is nothing." Tossing her head, Meghan shrugged his hand off. "We have nothing, 'Nick.' Our relationship is a lie based on a deception."

Closing his eyes, he pressed the heels of his palms against his temples and winced. "I really screwed up. How can I make it up to you?"

She dropped her chin, suddenly overcome by fatigue. What she needed was some time alone and a good long cry. Her throat ached as she forced the words past. "Right now, I just want you to go."

"I STILL CAN'T BELIEVE he did it." Meghan stood at the kitchen counter, helping Julie prepare Thursday night dinner.

"Well, what did you expect?"

"He just walked out, without another word."

"That's what you told him to do." Jules dropped the sliced vegetables into a pot of boiling water.

She thought about last night, the truth she'd discovered about his job. "He knows all about me now and I hardly know him at all."

"Why do you need to know anything? You just wanted to use his body for your personal pleasure and then leave, remember?"

She whipped around, ready to argue, until she saw that Julie was teasing. "I was wrong, you were right. Okay?"

"So, are you going to forgive him?"

"Eventually." Meghan took the Parmesan cheese from the refrigerator and began grating it into a bowl. "I've waited my whole life for him. I've never felt so fulfilled, so desired. Nick is funny and charming. He's intelligent and dynamic and—"

"You're in love with him!" Julie stared at her in wonder.

She sighed and set the cheese on the table. "This morning I wouldn't have hesitated to agree. But now..." She shrugged, not sure what she was feeling now. "Three or four earth-shattering orgasms aren't enough to build a lasting relationship on."

"It's one hell of a start." Her sister grinned wickedly.

"It all happened so fast. I'm afraid that in the throes of passion I confused lust with something deeper."

Julie began coating the fettuccine with olive oil and fresh herbs. "Sometimes two people just click, even though it seems reckless and hasty. Nick obviously makes you happy, both in bed and out. Maybe you should ignore logic and follow your instincts."

Meghan dropped her gaze while she opened the wine. "I don't know if I can trust my instincts, Jules. I've been wrong before."

"Why do you think he finally admitted he had the journal?"

"I don't know."

Jules refused to let her off the hook. "Yes, you do. He fell in love with you. He believes you love him enough to forgive everything he's done. Listen to the little voice inside you, Megs. I think it's telling you Nick is the one."

"FRANKIE RAMOS APPROACHED ME down by the pool this morning."

Alex's fingers clenched around the phone receiver. He was glad to hear Meghan's voice, but her words made his heart twist along with his gut. "Don't say anything else. Meet me down in the lobby in ten minutes."

He hung up before she could argue. He'd swept his rooms for listening devices, but since Ramos had located "Elise," he'd have to check her suite for bugs, too.

Great. Just goddamned great.

He paged Emelio and briefly explained what went down in the restaurant last night. After agreeing to meet in Emelio's suite, Alex headed for the door, still cursing under his breath. The elevator arrived just as an older couple walked up. His rotten mood must have shown on his face. They looked at him and obviously decided to wait for the next one.

Dammit! He should have figured Ramos would contact her. Meghan would probably use this as an excuse to break things off for good. When she admitted she loved him, he had figured they could find a way to be together in Miami. Now, who the hell knew.

He'd slept alone last night—one of the longest nights of his life. When he wasn't visited by nightmares, he'd been plagued by guilt and an overwhelming sense of loss. He didn't want what they had to be destroyed by his stupid mistake.

He was willing to give her some space, some time to cool down. But no way was he going to call it quits. Women like Meghan came around only once in a lifetime. If a guy was lucky.

The elevator doors slid open on the sixth floor and there she was. Her hair was tousled in soft waves and her face was bare. She was back to wearing her own clothes—a plain blue T-shirt and knee-length beige skirt. Behind her glasses, gray shadows circled her eyes. He guessed she didn't sleep well either.

Refusing to meet his gaze, Meghan crossed her arms and stepped inside. Turning, she stared up at the lighted numbers above the door. He might as well have been carpet lint for all the attention she paid him.

"Are you going to talk to me?"

"Hello, Alex. How are you?" Her casually polite tone couldn't hide the fatigue in her voice.

"Miserable. Lonely. Apologetic."

"Good." She finally looked at him.

He sighed, rubbing his fingers over the scar on his temple. Forgiveness wasn't going to come easy. "How are *you?*"

"Lonely. Miserable."

He smiled and reached for her hand. "You forgive me."

"I'm working on it." She accepted his touch then shifted away, a slight frown creasing her forehead. "How did Ramos find me?"

He dropped his hand to his side, reined in the irritation and hurt of her rejection. "Not sure. Emelio thinks he probably has people watching the resort."

"Oh, come on, Alex. How in the world could anyone find me in this place?"

"You're unforgettable, Meghan."

She must have taken his heartfelt statement for sarcasm because she dropped her gaze. Hunching her shoulders, she hugged her arms tighter around her waist. "Am I in danger?"

"No." His tone was emphatic. "I'll make sure nothing happens to you."

She slid a glance over at him, but said nothing.

That really pissed him off. Okay, he'd screwed up with the journal. But one thing he couldn't stand was the silent treatment. "Say something, dammit."

"You don't want anyone to overhear us discussing your case in the elevator."

"Then let's talk about us, Trouble."

Alex reached out and slapped his palm against the emergency stop button. The alarm rang and the elevator jerked hard. Off balance, Meghan threw her arms out as she fell into him. He grasped her elbow to steady her, then turned her until she faced him.

"Tell me you forgive me."

She sighed heavily. "I'm more embarrassed now than angry. You know all of my secrets and that makes me vulnerable."

"Very few people wouldn't have been tempted to read an open book, sweetheart."

"I guess."

Alex slid his hands down her arms to grasp her fingers. "Think about it. If the situation was reversed, wouldn't you at least glance at *my* journal?"

She arched one brow and pursed her lips. "I wouldn't keep it and then lie about having it."

He winced. "Yeah. That was kind of low."

"Once I had a chance to calm down, I started thinking. You could have kept my diary and I'd never have known." Meghan stepped in close, pressing her body against him. "Or you could have returned it right away and we'd have missed out on some incredible experiences."

Man, he hoped all this pelvic friction meant she'd forgiven him. Arousal raised the temperature inside the small elevator by several degrees. "Soo...you're saying you forgive me, right?"

"I'm saying, I know you were sincerely trying to please me." Her hips bumped the placket of his jeans. Again.

"And did I?" He cocked one eyebrow and laced his tone with innuendo.

A pretty blush stained her cheeks and her lips curled into a teasing smile. "You did okay, I guess."

He felt her shiver beneath his hands, heard her quick intake of breath, saw her whiskey-colored eyes lose their glacial reserve. The spicy floral scent of her skin caused a rush of longing so fierce, it almost brought him to his knees.

"I missed you, Trouble."

"We just saw each other twenty-six hours and forty-three minutes ago."

"Not that you were counting or anything." He grinned.

Sparks of awareness arced between them and he wasn't sure who moved first. He leaned down as she skimmed her hands up his chest and wrapped them around his neck. His mouth covered hers hungrily, and she surrendered to his kiss.

Alex backed her into the corner, his hands gripping her hips, and held her soft body to his hardening one. Her nipples peaked against his chest when she rubbed across the front of his jeans.

She felt so good, so right. And he loved her so much.

He raised one hand to the supple flesh of her breast, stroking her through the cotton fabric. She tangled her fingers in his hair, cradling his head, and deepened the kiss with a moan. Then the alarm rang again.

Alex broke their kiss as the elevator jerked into motion. He peered over at the descending numbers above the door. The maintenance crew must have overridden the emergency stop.

"So, was that what you wanted to talk about?" Meghan asked.

Alex looked down at her and grinned. Humor danced in her eyes as she smoothed a hand over her T-shirt, tucking it securely into her skirt.

"No, but I liked this conversation better than the one I was planning." There was nothing he wanted more than to go back upstairs and continue their discussion. But he was in enough trouble with Emelio and they needed to know Ramos's plans.

"My partner's waiting."

"RAMOS CAME UP TO ME out of nowhere."

"Where was this?" Emelio leaned forward in his seat.

Alex answered before Meghan could. "Down by the pool. Have we got anyone who can check out the resort staff?"

"I'll get somebody on it. What happened next, Meghan?"

"I was stunned to see him at first. Then he called me 'Mistress Elise' and I settled right into the role. It was weird." She made a puzzled expression. "Anyway, he said he was glad he found me. He wanted to make arrangements for this bizarre request he whispered in my ear last night.''

Em gave her a quizzical look, but she shook her head. "You don't really want to know."

Alex shifted around on the sofa until Meghan reached over to take his hand. He probably didn't want to know either. It would just give him another excuse to put Ramos in the ground.

Emelio glanced at their joined hands and frowned. He sat back in the chair, hooking his thumbs into his pockets. "What else?"

"I pretended 'Elise' was looking forward to acting out his fantasy. I kind of toyed with him, trying to keep him talking. Basically, he wanted to make sure I'd be in the casino tonight."

He couldn't handle this. The very idea of her going head to head with Ramos was making him sweat. Alex scowled, pissed off at both the situation and his own anxiety. "Yeah, well, he's going to be disappointed when you don't show up. If I let you go—"

"What do you mean, 'if you let me'?" Meghan turned to look at him, brows drawn. "I have to be there. He's expecting me."

"Forget it. No way."

"Hang on, partner," Emelio interrupted, trying to get him to see reason. "We need her to do more and you know it. If Ramos confessed his secret sex fantasies to 'Elise,' who knows what else he might tell her?"

"Men like Frankie Ramos don't talk business with high-priced working girls."

Crossing her arms, she shot back, "Well, he's not

willing to talk business with *you*. Ramos wants 'Elise' to come without 'Nick.'"

Emelio interrupted again. "Alex, man, he might relax with her, reveal something we can use to finally nail him to the wall."

There had to be another way. The last thing he wanted was to put her in danger again. But, dammit, she did need to be there. "Fine. You can drape yourself all over me and look pretty. Nothing more."

"Sorry to disappoint you, Stud-muffin, but this arm ornament has a brain." Meghan tapped her nails against his thigh to get his attention. "He never questioned anything I said, so I know I did a good job of playing him. It's obvious 'Elise' intrigues him. If she drapes herself all over *him*, she can keep track of who he talks to and what he does."

Alex patted his shirt pockets, looking for his cigarettes. Shit. He'd left them back in his suite. "I don't like the way you're talking about 'Elise' like she's a different person."

"I *am* a different person than I was five days ago." She spoke quietly but there was an edge to her tone.

He closed his eyes, knowing what had to be done and hating it. A muzzle flash. A sharp crack of sound. Pain. The nausea threatened to choke him as he looked at her. "Why would you even want to do this?"

"I'm doing it for Kyle. And for Greg. And for us."

He lifted their joined hands, pressed her wrist against his cheek. He had no choice but to nod once in agreement. Meghan smiled and leaned over to kiss him. She had a way of making him feel like the only man in the world. It would kill him if anything happened to her.

"Put your hormones on hold—both of you—and

let's close this case.'' Em glanced at his watch. "We've got people and equipment to coordinate, partner. And not much time to do it. Meghan, we'll see you tonight before you go to the casino."

"I still don't like this one damned bit, hombre."

"Like it or not, we can't let this opportunity pass."

MEGHAN CHECKED HER APPEARANCE in the bathroom mirror. Elise was a risk-taker, daring and seductive. She liked her champagne cold and her men hot. Tonight she would be stepping out of the diary and into the fire.

Nervous excitement had butterflies tickling her stomach. She knew exactly what she had to do tonight and how. She'd get Ramos comfortable, persuade him to drop his guard. Then, if she played him like she did this morning, he'd be eating out of her hand and talking about his business in no time.

Meghan continued to stare at her reflection. Jules had loaned her a peach satin evening gown. The dress was simply cut but snuggled every curve. One seam was split to mid-thigh and the deep neckline showed off her cleavage. Love that Wonderbra.

She heard fingers drum against the front door. She winked at the mirror then went to let Alex in, the hem of her dress fluttering around her ankles as she moved. She swung the door open and her heart turned over.

He looked so handsome, so very sexy in the tuxedo he'd worn the first night they made love. His damp hair was swept back from his face in dark waves. His usual confident posture and flirtatious attitude were absent, though. She stood aside to let him pass and saw the small bag from the resort gift shop.

"What's that?"

Instead of a present, Alex pulled out a flat black case and some dangling wires with a small disc on the end. "This is a body mike. Emelio should be here in a minute to make sure it transmits properly."

She followed him into the living room, eyeing the device warily. She didn't like the idea of having to censor every word for the rest of the night. "Are you going to wear it or am I?"

"It's for you. I can't take the chance of Ramos deciding to frisk me. Turn around."

Meghan hesitated with a slight frown, then did as he asked. His hand brushed over her back as he undid the hook fastening the top of the gown and slid the zipper down. He slipped his hand inside to secure the transmitter at her waist.

Her skin tingled everywhere he touched, his warm fingers sending tremors along her nerves. She didn't know anything about body mikes, but he sure seemed to be taking his time attaching the mike to her body. Not that she minded.

Gently nudging her shoulder, Alex turned her around to face him. She heard his breath hitch, saw his pupils dilate when he looked down. The sagging bodice of her gown revealed the lace demi-bra that barely covered her breasts. Her taut nipples were visible through the sheer material.

He cleared his throat and exhaled slowly. His fingers traced her collarbone then glided along her chest, leaving a trail of tingling heat in their wake. Finally, he slipped two fingers under the front clasp of her bra, taping the small microphone between her breasts.

"How does that feel?" His smoke-roughened voice was soft and sensual.

"Wonderful... I mean, fine."

Her heart beat an unsteady tattoo and heat rushed between her thighs. Alex took a step closer and reached around her back to zip up the gown. When he ducked his head, she pressed a kiss against his neck. His breath ruffled her hair. The casual intimacy sent her pulse racing.

He angled his head to look down at her. She returned his gaze, saw the love and the lust mingling there. Their bodies drew inexorably closer. His hands encircled her waist and she placed her fingers on his forearms. Meghan's lips parted even as Alex began to lower his head.

A sharp rap at the door broke the spell. He held her stare for a few seconds and she saw her frustration and regret mirrored in his light green eyes. She inhaled deeply and tried to get her chaotic hormones under control. They didn't have time. "Go let Emelio in while I fix my lipstick."

"It's not too late to back out, Meghan. We can do this without you."

"No, you can't, 'Nick.' *We* have a bad guy to trap."

15

There's no excitement in my life. I've always been the responsible, respectable, reliable one. Just once, I'd like to do something impulsive, maybe even a little dangerous....

SHOW TIME.

A surge of adrenaline raced through Alex's veins. His heart thundered in his chest and he felt light-headed. He clenched his jaw when the nausea hit. Like a warrior preparing for battle, he tried to still his mind and yet remain alert to his surroundings.

Inside the Cayo Sueño Casino, slot machines jingled and clanged, and smoke from expensive cigars wafted toward the ceiling. Bright, multi-hued lights illuminated the tastefully decorated gaming hall. The low murmur of voices filled the casino full of people praying for Lady Luck's blessing.

He usually got a rush out of situations like this, adrenaline being his drug of choice. He relished the surprise and the unknown. Now he dreaded pitting his wits, as well as his limited gaming skills, against Ramos and the others sure to be here, because something too precious depended on his performance: Meghan's safety.

With effort, Alex yanked on the role he needed to play. Okay. His name was Nick Alexander. He was a finance geek. Confident, self-assured, jaded. Slightly arrogant look and attitude. A successful investment broker.

Striding through the casino, his eyes scanned the crowd. Concentrate on the faces. Forget the nausea, catalogue the players. He did nothing to indicate he knew the blackjack dealer across the way. Emelio glanced over and caught his eye, but didn't acknowledge him either.

After stopping a waitress to order a beer, Alex headed for the cashier's desk. He put on a professional smile, Nick's smile, for the busty redhead behind the window. "Evening. I'd like to establish a line of credit."

"Certainly, sir. I'm sure you're good for it." She offered him a wink and a flirtatious grin.

He pretended to laugh at her joke as he pulled out a wallet full of hundred-dollar bills. He chose the platinum card for which a special debit account had been set up and passed it across the counter.

"How much would you like to start with, sir?"

"Fifty thousand."

The redhead didn't blink. She simply ran his card through a scanner and selected a stack of chips in one-thousand-dollar denominations.

"Thanks." Alex took the tray of fifty chips and started to turn when the redhead touched his arm.

"If you're not doing anything later—"

He shook his head and smiled to soften his refusal. "Sorry. I've made other plans."

Before Meghan, the generously endowed and scantily clad cashier might have easily found her way into his bed. Now, he had no interest in the woman or what she offered. Unfortunately, the woman he *was* interested in hadn't completely forgiven him yet.

Since his first marriage broke up, he'd avoided any kind of commitment. It was just easier to be alone when he could never be sure where—or who—he'd be from week to week. Meghan made him realize what was missing from his life, how empty it was.

Whatever it took, he planned to have a future with her. The only thing he wanted more than seeing Ramos behind bars was seeing Meghan's face across the pillows every morning.

Ramos stood to greet him as he approached a table set apart from the rest. "Nick. I began to think you were not coming."

Yeah, right. No way in hell would he miss an opportunity to figure out how the money laundering operation worked. "How could I resist the chance to take your assets?"

Ramos's laugh was too loud, too harsh. Studying his adversary, Alex realized the man was under the influence. His pupils were so dilated that his eyes appeared black. So the rumors were true. Ramos wasn't just sampling his product; he was overindulging. That would make him more unpredictable than ever tonight.

Anxiety clawed at him. It clutched at his throat, tore at his gut. Meghan was counting on him. Just like Greg had looked to him for guidance and his ex-wife, Liz, had hoped for his affection. And Emelio had relied on his judgment in Overtown.

All of his life, people had expected things from him and somehow he'd failed to measure up... Not this time. Meghan's safety depended on his ability to bait and trap Ramos. No matter what, he wouldn't let her down. An odd sense of calm settled over him, like he'd reached the eye of the storm in his mind. His anxiety evaporated and the nausea passed as ''Nick'' met Ramos's stare.

''I had some personal business to take care of first.''

''The best kind of business, I see.'' Ramos removed a white handkerchief from his jacket, indicating a spot on the side of Alex's neck.

How did Meghan's lipstick get on him? He wiped the handkerchief along his throat, but nothing came off on the cloth. Aw, hell. The color on his skin was a love bite from the night before.

Ramos let out a dry rasp of false humor. ''The lady has left her mark on you, my friend.''

Alex bared his teeth, letting the other man draw his own conclusions. ''That's what she gets paid to do.''

''Elise is not with you?'' With a show of looking around, the bastard tried to goad him.

''Not anymore.'' He pretended to hesitate, letting disappointment sharpen his tone. ''Our business is finished.''

Ramos gave him a thin, satisfied smile, then indicated the empty seat at the table. ''Shall we proceed?''

''Will Señor Braga be joining us?''

''Rogelio has been...unavoidably detained.''

Alex gave no outward sign of his reaction. Did that mean Braga was conducting some business or that Ramos had him murdered? He suddenly wished for that damned body mike so Emelio could try to find out.

In the meantime, he shook hands with the four men seated at the table. He'd just placed his chips on the table and taken his seat when the pretty blond waitress brought his beer.

"Thanks, babe. Don't let any of these glasses go empty." "Nick" tucked a hundred-dollar bill into her cleavage. Ramos nodded in approval.

Ogling the waitress's legs as she walked away, the men passed several moments with idle boasts about stock trades and lies about women. Once the small talk was exhausted, the dealer began shuffling cards. Each of the players threw his thousand-dollar ante into the pot.

Alex lit a cigarette and studied his hand. Not bad. Not bad at all. He was more than pleased to see the queen of clubs and the queen of hearts among them. The latter reminded him of Meghan and he glanced over at the entrance. As if he'd willed her presence, she walked in.

The sight of her had the same impact as the first time they'd met. Despite the danger they were facing, primal lust grabbed him by the—wait. She seemed nervous, uncertain. Her fingers toyed with the bracelet on her wrist. Only Meghan did that, not "Elise."

Alex sighed. She'd done a great job the other night when impulse and instinct guided her. Now, though, Meghan was fully aware of what she'd gotten herself into. He desperately wanted to take her in his arms and walk her right back out the door. But he knew how the game had to play out.

Her eyes scanned the room, searching. The instant she focused on him, an expression of glad relief crossed her face. She winked at him and threw her shoulders back, suddenly looking bolder, a little more cynical and a lot more confident.

Alex watched her transformation with reluctant admiration.

With a poised and determined stride, "Elise" sauntered through the casino. Ramos must have seen her, too, because he quickly excused himself from his guests.

With lightning speed, Alex's mind conjured up, and just as rapidly discarded, several lame excuses to follow. Trusting Meghan to pull off the charade again was taxing every instinct he had.

He deliberately unclenched his jaw. *Relax. Watch the game.* The play moved quickly since everyone at the table except him seemed to be getting bad hands. He was only down a few thousand dollars, but the others had dropped at least a hundred grand in record time.

During the next few deals, he noticed the other players bet too heavily, considering their losses. And they were using the one-thousand-dollar chips. The tray of ten-thousand-dollar chips in front of Ramos's seat hadn't been touched.

"Is it just me or has Lady Luck abandoned us tonight?"

Alex looked over at the man who'd spoken. He was surprised to see that, despite the question, Shelton was in a good mood. Especially for a guy who'd lost forty thousand dollars just in the last hand.

One of the other players, Kent, laughed and slapped Shelton on the back. "I have a feeling she'll be back to visit us soon."

Some instinct set off warning bells in the back of Alex's subconscious. "You sound awfully certain about that."

Shelton gave him a sharp look before he dropped his

gaze to focus on his cards. Kent laughed again. "Take it easy. Braga told me Nick here is our newest banker. Let him in on the joke."

Kent showed his cards. He had a straight flush with face cards. What the hell? Shelton turned over a four-of-a-kind and the other players had similar good cards. These guys were losing on purpose. Alex shot a glance at the tray of ten-thousand dollar chips. Jackpot.

The profits from the drug sales were being washed, dried, starched and pressed right here in the casino.

ATTITUDE.

It was all about the attitude and, oh baby, did she have that. She was mysterious, intelligent and sexy. Everything a man could want. Ramos didn't stand a chance. "Elise" ate guys like him for breakfast and still had room for a snack before lunch.

Meghan leaned forward, resting one arm along the table's edge. She tilted her head invitingly and smiled. "So...you'd like to enjoy my company for a while. I have to tell you, Frankie, I'm very particular when choosing my associations."

"I applaud your discretion." Ramos sat across from her with his back to the bar. He had demanded the best bottle of champagne available and then proceeded to gulp it down like water. Judging by his wild hand motions and animated expressions, he was more than drunk.

"Tell me, what attracts a woman like you, Mistress Elise?"

She immediately thought of Alex. His sexy laugh, his easy charm, his tender affection. She knew he was close by, but for now she was on her own. "Elise" traced her middle finger in lazy circles around the rim of her champagne flute, pleased to see Ramos's eyes follow the movement.

"Every man is different. What turns me on isn't easy to define or explain."

"I can't help but wonder how Nick Alexander was able to hold your interest." He finished his champagne, refilled it from the second bottle and topped off her glass.

She shook her head coyly, her tone reproachful. "My former patrons, and what I may have done to them, shouldn't concern you. He was an amusing diversion, but now I'm looking to move on. I'm wondering whether *you* have what it takes to keep me interested."

"You're already interested, my dear. Otherwise you would not have accepted my invitation."

"I'll admit to being curious about you." She dipped her index finger into the champagne and slowly raised it to her mouth. Holding his gaze, she licked the wine from her fingertip.

"I am a very important man." He puffed out his chest and sat a bit taller in his seat. "More successful and more powerful than Alexander will ever be."

That was the third or fourth time he'd mentioned Nick. It was getting tiresome and the tape securing the microphone between her breasts had begun to itch. Maybe she needed to kick her attitude up a notch.

"Really, Francisco. If I agree to take you on, you'll have to convince me that you're worth my time." She cast him a condescending glare. "I'm beginning to have my doubts."

Violent anger flashed across his face, giving him a

crazed look. His mood had swung 180 degrees in a matter of seconds. "Francisco Guillermo Ramos is not a man to be trifled with. Do you think you can toy with me, Elise?"

Sticking pins in his overinflated ego had been too tempting to resist. Meghan casually lowered her eyes, pretending to inspect her manicure. Maybe she should have resisted? *No. Don't back down.*

"I know I can toy with you, Frankie. That's what you offered to pay me for."

After a beat, he laughed heartily and she knew she was still in control. "Business. This, I understand."

"Hmm, yes, you would, wouldn't you?" Time to wind him a little tighter around her finger. "A man of your reputation, a man with power and success. Maybe you can help me with a small problem."

His dark eyes glittered from more than the effects of the wine. "Perhaps we can help each other. My advice in exchange for your services."

She angled her head, making sure Emelio was still at the blackjack table to her left. He nodded and smiled briefly. *Here goes.* Meghan arched her back slightly to expose more cleavage, batted her lashes and pretended to confide in him.

"One of my clients can be rather talkative, given the proper motivation." She wiggled her brows, but left the details to his imagination. "I took advantage of some information he let slip. Now I have a large sum of money I'd rather not give to the Internal Revenue Service."

His tone was dismissive as Ramos emptied the second champagne bottle into their glasses. "Cash-based operations such as my vending machines, fast-food restaurants and pawnshops are quite efficient—''

She made a tsking sound as she reached for him, trailing her fingernails over his hand. When he looked up, she licked her lips slowly. "I need more than that, Frankie. If you really want me to perform the fantasy you requested, then I want help moving my funds offshore."

"I do not think—"

"Don't think. Imagine. Picture me doing all of the things you whispered in my ear. All of them. Twice."

Ramos swallowed visibly and shifted on his chair. "My money is structured into smaller amounts and placed in regular bank accounts. After that it is wired to my cousin as an overseas transfer."

Over Ramos's left shoulder, Meghan saw Alex walk up to the bar. She noticed him look toward Emelio, then grin. It seemed "Elise" was getting the evidence they were after. He made a circular motion with his index finger to keep Frankie talking.

Under the table, she slid her foot up and down his leg. She tilted her chin to one side and squeezed his hand suggestively. "What happens to the money after that?"

"Here is the brilliant part, Elise. Cousin Pablo has set up special accounts for 'charitable donations.'" He named a South American children's organization.

Meghan's nails dug into his hand before she could hide her dismay. *You son of a—* She'd given those frauds a hundred bucks last year! Now she knew the money went into Ramos's pockets instead of a hungry child's stomach.

He kept talking, as if the more he told "Elise," the

more she'd do to him later. He clutched at her hand, but she slid her fingers away. Unable to stand the sight of him, she looked over at the bar.

Alex had been nursing a bottle of beer while keeping his eyes on Emelio. All of a sudden, she saw him break into a wide smile of triumph. He casually reached up with his left hand to twist the diamond stud in his ear. That was the signal for her to, as he'd put it, "get the hell out of the way."

"Well, I'm very impressed, Frankie." Mission accomplished, she gripped her evening bag and stood up. Moving to the right of her chair, she gave him a coy smile. "I need to powder my nose, but I'd like to hear more when I get back."

She'd taken only a few steps toward Alex when the casino erupted into chaos. Emelio came rushing around from the blackjack table, bellowing, "Freeze!" More than a dozen law enforcement agents seemed to appear from thin air, shouting commands and waving badges.

Someone screamed, a tray of glassware shattered, a woman fainted and casino patrons tried to scramble out of the way. Ramos twisted in his chair and called out. "Come back, Elise. I'll protect you!"

She turned at the sound of his voice, not sure which way to move to avoid getting trampled. The federal agents were converging from all directions and she really didn't want to get caught in the middle.

Ramos had sobered up immediately, his eyes wild as he took in the pandemonium. Then his gaze narrowed dangerously as he focused beyond her. Uh-oh.

Some of Alex's satisfaction must have shown on his face because Ramos scowled at him in utter fury. Meghan knew the instant Frankie realized he'd been set up. She saw the sickened disbelief in his eyes as he knocked over the chair and leapt to his feet.

She watched in horror as he reached under his jacket and freed his gun from its holster. "No!" she screamed.

Ramos pointed it directly at Alex's chest. "*Hijo de perra!* This time I will not miss."

This can't happen again. I won't let it! With no thought for her own safety, Meghan spread her arms to block his aim. She felt Alex tackle her from behind, his shoulder slamming into her back. The force knocked the air from her lungs and the momentum swept them to the floor.

Pain. Burning pain. The top of her right shoulder was on fire. When she looked, she saw that blood ran down her arm. As she got her wind back, she swallowed hard against the bile rising in her throat.

"Oh my God, sweetheart. You're hit!"

Alex pulled a white handkerchief from his pocket and pressed it firmly to her arm. He kissed her temple as she winced in pain. "Hey! Somebody call 9-1-1. We need an ambulance!"

She held tightly to him, trying not to black out from shock and adrenaline overload. Alex shifted his weight and helped her to sit up. She looked over to see Emelio plant a foot on Ramos and wrest the gun away from him.

"Francisco Ramos. You're under arrest for assault with a deadly weapon, drug distribution and conspiracy to launder drug money. You have the right to remain silent—"

"You have nothing on me, *pendejo*. My lawyer will eat your badge for lunch."

Emelio smirked. "Tell him to get in line."

Alex kept the handkerchief tight against Meghan's shoulder, his other arm wrapped anxiously around her. Then he closed his eyes since all he could see was white dancing spots anyway. His brain had shut down when he saw Ramos fire his Glock 29.

Willing his pulse to even out, he lifted the cloth to take a look at the wound. It seemed like a through-and-through, a nasty graze across the top of her shoulder. "Dammit! Where's that ambulance?"

She clutched at him with trembling hands, whispering his name over and over again. Blood soaked through the handkerchief, staining his hand. An ache like nothing he'd ever felt before squeezed his chest in a cruel vise. He'd endangered Meghan for the sake of the job.

She'd handled the con flawlessly from the start, but he knew exactly what the effort had cost her. The stress of having to process every action through an assumed identity showed on her face, as did the pain of the gunshot wound. His breathing was as shallow as hers and his hand shook as he cupped her cheek.

"Julie's going to be mad that I ruined her dress." She laughed shakily, eyes much too bright for his liking. Her face was ghostly pale and her body quivered uncontrollably.

"You saved my life." More than that, she'd saved his soul. Alex gazed into her whiskey-colored eyes, his heart full of gratitude and love. He'd been half-alive before he met her, drifting through a lonely existence, not understanding what was missing. Now that he'd found her, he'd never let her go.

"You're lucky I didn't shoot you myself." There

was an hysterical edge to her voice. "What were you thinking, you lunatic, standing there grinning like an idiot?"

"I was just so damned proud of you." Her eyes were glazing over. He had to keep her awake so he kept talking. "Thanks to your quick thinking, Ramos is finally going to prison. You really had him convinced Elise was for real."

She winced when he increased the pressure on her shoulder. Meghan couldn't see that the graze was still bleeding. "Of course he was convinced. I was good."

Alex chuckled humorlessly. "You were amazing. If you ever want a job—"

"That is not even remotely funny."

"I know it's not—I'm sorry." His fingers caressed her hair as he forced the words past the tightness in his throat. "You were so brave—and you must have been terrified."

"I must have been crazy."

"Yeah, crazy about me. I love you, Trouble."

An odd expression crossed her face. Some instinct told him it wasn't due to the bullet wound. "Alex—"

Just then one of his fellow agents came up behind them and pulled him away. He spoke in an undertone. "I'm gonna search you for weapons. Try not to enjoy this, big guy."

"In your dreams, Sandalis. You're not my type." He mumbled the reply under his breath. Shelton and Kent were both watching, so he couldn't risk breaking cover.

As one of the agents dragged Ramos off, he stared at Alex with hard black eyes. "You will pay for this! We have not seen the last of each other."

"You've got to stop watching rerun episodes of that *Miami Vice* show, Frankie."

Just then, cold steel handcuffs were snapped around his wrists. Enough curious bystanders whispered and pointed to make him momentarily forget he worked for the good guys. Worst of all was the look of dismay on Meghan's face.

"What happens now, Alex?" she murmured.

The underlying question punched a hole in his gut. She wasn't talking about the moment; she was asking about their future. He saw the withdrawal in her expression, but there was nothing he could do about it right now. So he kept his tone light and smiled.

"We'll put on a good show for the other suspects, then I'll slip over to the DEA's Post of Duty Office. I have a ton of reports to type out, but I'll come see you as soon as I can."

Emelio walked over and helped Meghan stand up. "The paramedics are here. I'll have somebody go with you to the hospital so you can get that shoulder looked at." He glanced at Alex and spoke under his breath. "Don't worry. I'll check on her myself as soon as we get this squared away."

"I owe you one," he replied in an equally low tone.

"Let's go, scumbag! You're under arrest." Special Agent Sandalis raised his voice and shoved Alex forward.

As "Nicholas Alexander" was taken into custody and informed of his rights, he saw Meghan's eyes cloud with emotion a second before she turned away.

16

My dream vacation has turned into a nightmare of danger and deception. I found love only to discover I can't live with it....

"MORE?"

"Yes, ma'am. And I'm pretty sure this isn't all." The porter gave her a crooked grin as he handed Meghan yet another bouquet of flowers. "Whoever he is, he must be real sorry."

She closed the door and walked past the suitcases lined up in the foyer. In the living room, vases and baskets of bright, fragrant blooms covered almost every surface. The flowers had been arriving all morning. After making a place for the lilies on the coffee table, she went back out to the balcony. The overwhelming aroma of all those flowers wouldn't choke her here.

She picked up her pen and continued writing where she'd left off.

I wanted to be someone different. I wanted to have an adventure. What's that old saying? About being careful what you wish for? Too bad I had to get shot to realize the truth—"Elise" is a part of me, not a different self, but in the end, I'm still

Meghan. The responsible, respectable, reliable one.

I started the week wanting a fling. Now I want a forever. But it won't be with Nick, my fantasy come true. And it won't be with Alex the undercover agent. How could a man who thrives on danger, who has a different name for each day of the week, commit to forever?

DRAWING THE BACK OF HER HAND under her chin, Meghan wiped away the beaded perspiration. What had possessed her to trek out to the east end of Cayo Sueño in this heat? The air felt sultry and still. Not a cloud appeared in the deep blue sky. The late Saturday-morning temperature must have reached the upper nineties already.

She adjusted the weight of the tote on her good shoulder, absently listening to the lecture on the pre-Columbian ruin. The excavated stone walls contrasted starkly against the lush foliage and murky water of the salt ponds.

"Researchers are divided in their opinions of the stone circle's origin. Some think it was carved by a breakaway band of Maya from the Yucatan Peninsula across the Gulf. Others believe it's the foundation of a Tequesta Indian building. However, both sides agree that this site was an important ceremonial center of worship."

Meghan peered at her watch as the lecturer droned on about the size and symmetry of the ceremonial circle. Suddenly her vision blurred and she felt dizzy. Realizing she was getting dehydrated, she opened a bottle of water and drank half of it down in a few gulps.

"I'll take some of that, if you don't mind." Alex appeared at her side, brushing a forearm across his brow.

She greeted him with a faltering smile, more pleased than she cared to admit that he'd sought her out. Handing him the water, she took the opportunity to admire his long, tanned legs. She avoided looking at his shirt. Today's "fashion don't" had multicolored parrots and palm trees.

"Are you doing okay, sweetheart?"

She started to shrug, then winced at the twinge in her right shoulder. "I'm tired and a little out of it from the meds they gave me at the hospital."

"Sorry I didn't make it over to see you. I had a ton of reports to fill out and some other stuff to take care of."

"You didn't miss much. They just bandaged me up, and then Julie brought me back. She was more upset than I was."

While the lecturer continued, Alex leaned close to whisper playfully in her ear. "This is boring. Want to cut class?"

The idea of sneaking off to make love in the foliage was tempting. Very tempting. But not meant to be. She maintained a light tone until she could talk to him alone. "Would you believe, I've never skipped before? I had a perfect attendance record all through school."

"In that case, let's walk on the wild side."

At the start of her vacation, Meghan thought she wanted to do just that. She remembered the moment they met, the first spark of awareness, the first feeling of connection. In that instant, she'd somehow known he would change her life. But she'd discovered that acting wild had consequences.

Alex led her away from the tour group, past a pair of researchers inspecting the rocks and dirt, to the far side of the excavation site. She dropped her tote bag to the ground and climbed one of the rocks.

Now distanced from the voices and the hammering, Meghan could hear the waves rolling onto the beach and the wind in the tree branches. The slight breeze, carrying the scent of sunlight and flowers, ruffled her hair.

Alex boosted himself up beside her on the limestone wall, elbows locked at his sides and legs dangling over the edge. Squinting against the sun's glare, he dipped his head to indicate the weathered stones around them. "Greg would have loved this."

She didn't want to discuss Greg. They needed to talk about the present, not the past. Then again, maybe this was a good opening. "Really? Why?"

"He wanted to be an archeologist when he grew up. That kid was crazy about dinosaurs and fossils." Alex chuckled, apparently enjoying a particular memory. "I remember one time Greg found these old bones in the backyard. Guess he must have been around ten. He was so excited—totally convinced he'd found some prehistoric skeleton. I didn't have the heart to tell him it was probably the family pet of a previous owner."

She pushed her glasses back onto her nose and gazed at him thoughtfully, feeling a mix of pride and pity toward him. "How much longer are you going to punish yourself? How long before you realize you can't save him?"

His light green eyes widened in shock, then he

clenched his jaw and looked away without a reply. She'd hurt him, but she'd wanted to make a point. She softened her tone, knowing it wouldn't soften the blow. "I'm glad you're here, Alex. I can say goodbye in person."

"There's plenty of time to talk about that. We don't leave until tomorrow afternoon."

"I'm leaving today."

"What? Wait a—"

"I wish you well, Alex, but it's over between us."

He regarded her through hooded eyes and his voice took on a bitter edge. "You're throwing away our happiness because of something in the past. There's no reason—"

"The past *is* the reason." She held his gaze, needing him to understand. "I saw what Julie went through, always waiting for a call in the middle of the night or a knock at the door."

"That won't—" He tried to slip his left arm around her waist, but she shifted away to stop him.

"Yes. It will." Meghan spoke softly, but her tone was certain. "Because you're fighting a battle you can't win, and you don't seem to care who gets in the way."

His features took on a defensive expression. "It was never my intention to hurt you. God knows, I never intended for you to be hurt by anyone else, either."

She gave him a hard stare. "You *knew* what kind of man Ramos was, what he was capable of. And you still let me walk into the firing line."

"As I remember it, you insisted on taking part. Besides, Emelio and I were there the whole time to protect you."

"You guys were there to make sure you got enough evidence to lock Ramos away."

"I was doing my job, the only way I know how." His wooden tone indicated that he'd withdrawn from her.

She couldn't really be angry with him. Kyle had been the same type of man—determined to take on the world and leave it better than he'd found it. But one cop with a penchant for danger was more than enough for her.

"I'm just saving myself from further harm, the only way *I* know how."

"Don't do this." His features were set as though etched in stone, but a hint of desperation colored his voice. "Don't throw away the best thing that ever happened to either one of us."

Meghan climbed down off the wall, feeling sad and resigned. "If this is the best thing, then the worst will be unbearable. You're not the kind of man I can plan a future with."

Alex jumped to his feet and stood before her. His dark brows slanted in a frown, his eyes insistent. "You have no idea what kind of man I am—"

"That's exactly the problem—"

"Because I had a role to play—"

She sobbed. "I don't know how—"

"Quit interrupting, will you!" He let out a harsh breath and tightly clenched one fist, as if reining in his emotions. "'Nicholas' is no more real than the dream lover you created in your journal."

"Well, since you brought up my diary..."

"Don't even go there, Trouble. I'm through apologizing. I can fulfill your fantasies, but I don't live my life as one.''

She whirled around. ''Excuse me? Alex or 'Nick' or whoever you are today, what is your whole life other than a fantasy?''

''And yours isn't? Until this week you've only lived inside the pages of your journal. Who's the real Meghan? Or should I call you 'Elise'?''

She huffed out a breath, acknowledging the truth of his question. ''I know I got myself into this with my stupid plan. And because I tried to be someone I'm not, I ended up falling in love with a man who doesn't exist.''

Alex turned her around to face him, taking care not to jar her shoulder, refusing to let go when she struggled. ''The woman you've been this week is closer to your true nature than you realize. You're impulsive and fun-loving and passionate—''

''I know you were attracted to 'Elise'—I saw it in your face and the gleam in your eyes. But that's not who I am.'' She finally freed herself from his grasp. ''Pretending to be Mata Hari was only fun until the bullets started flying.''

He reached over to grab her hand, entwining his fingers with hers. ''Give me another chance. I know we can work this out. We can get beyond the issue of my job.''

''There's also the issue of your integrity. How can I possibly trust a man who lies for a living?''

''I'm not the only one with an honesty problem.'' He squeezed her hand, frustration evident on his face. ''It's easier to make me the bad guy than face your fears and insecurities.''

She closed her eyes against the hurt in his expression. She was dying inside, but she just couldn't do this. She looked at him, silently begging him to understand. "I can't live with the risks, the chances you take, the constant danger."

He turned his face, but not before she saw the sheen of tears in his eyes. His smoke-roughened voice was quiet and firm, as though he refused to let it sound like begging.

"Don't leave me. Please."

Omigod. Her heart just crumbled into dust. It wouldn't be that hard to give in, to plan their lives around his secret assignments, but she was afraid. She wanted more than sex, more than seduction. She wanted the house and kids and dogs. And a husband who came home every night.

Alex wasn't destined to be her Mr. Fabulous. She needed a safe, dependable nine-to-five guy for a real relationship to be possible. He was more likely to work from 9:00 p.m. until 5:00 a.m., infiltrating cartels and lurking in dockyards.

It had been a thrilling and enlightening week. She'd wanted something more out of life, wanted to be someone different. She'd learned a lot about herself and she'd always be grateful to Nick—Alex for that. But the adventure had come to an end. No matter how wonderful he was in bed and how much fun he was out of it, he wasn't the right man for her.

"I don't need any more heroes in my life."

He clasped her hand and pulled her tightly into his arms.

Knowing it was a mistake, Meghan cursed her inability to resist him. She put her arms about his waist and, against her better judgment, relaxed into his embrace. Only for a moment, one last moment. For a long while they stood in silence, simply holding onto each other.

She felt the heat of his body through the ugly shirt and the tension in the muscles underneath. Pressing her mouth to the side of his neck, she could feel his pulse beating against her lips. It suddenly struck her how much she'd miss the smell of his skin.

"Kiss me goodbye, Trouble."

He tilted her chin and tenderly covered her mouth. His kiss tasted of sadness, of longing and of regret. When they parted, she was dazed by the depth of emotion she felt from him as well as within herself. Thinking of the old adage, she decided it *was* better never to have loved at all.

ALEX GLARED at the phone receiver in his hand, actually believing he could reach Meghan by sheer force of will. He'd been calling Julie's condo all week, but kept getting the answering machine. He had to talk to her. Hell, he just wanted to hear her voice.

He remained lost in thought until the nasal computer message instructed that if he'd like to place a call, please hang up and try again. Frustrated, he put down the phone and stared morosely at the carpet.

Loneliness was a dull constant ache in his chest. Meghan's face haunted his dreams, leaving him restless and miserable. He remembered how well her body fit with his, the sweetness of her kiss, the way she looked in the soft light of dusk and her soft cries that first night they'd made love.

Impatiently, he pulled his drifting thoughts together. Heaving himself up from the couch, he padded across the near-empty apartment. Walking into the sparse kitchen, he made a mental note to buy some furniture.

He had a king-size bed, the couch, a TV and a small dinette set. He kept meaning to put up some shades and a few pictures, but work had always demanded his time and attention. So, the walls remained blank and the windows were covered only by dust.

Alex scratched his bare chest with one hand and grabbed a cold beer out of the refrigerator with the other. He twisted off the cap and drank a third of the bottle down. The taste of bitterness remained. So did his restlessness.

He missed her desperately. Meghan had unwittingly shared the most intimate parts of herself with him, while he remained secretive and distant. No one had ever touched his heart like she did; he'd never allowed anyone close enough to try.

She was everything he never knew he needed.

He'd give anything to make amends, to have her trust again. Meghan's love was a precious gift and he wanted to be worthy of it. He wanted to see himself as the man reflected in her eyes.

Alex longed for a cigarette, but he'd finally given them up when she walked out on him. The smokes were part of his past; they had no place in his future—a future he hoped to share with the woman he loved. Leaving the unfinished beer on the counter, he went into the bedroom to put on a shirt. Then he scooped up his keys and headed for the DEA's Miami Field Office.

ALEX'S EARS WERE RINGING, his head ached, and he was going to need a new ass when his boss finished chewing on it.

"You screwed up royally by letting a civilian in on the investigation, Alex."

He slumped deeper into his chair while Brent Easton and the Internal Affairs investigator took turns beating up on him.

"And then, knowing you were wrong, you still stupidly and unnecessarily endangered the life of that civilian...."

When the Division Chief walked into Brent's office to add his two cents, Alex's day went from bad to worse. "As an eight-year veteran, you should have..."

He tuned out the ongoing reprimand. Looking back on those eight years, he didn't like what he saw. Subterfuge was a justifiable necessity of his profession. He never hesitated to do whatever it took to get a case off his desk and into court. He changed his personality along with his underwear if that's what got results.

For once, the success of an investigation wasn't worth the damaging effect on his personal life. Having to fight his fear and anxiety had distracted him from what should have been top priority.

Meghan could have died.

Envisioning the rest of his days without her, the thought spun around and around his mind. She'd risked everything for him and she could have died. Not only had the job cost him the woman he loved, it cost him his identity. There was no way he could do his job effectively anymore. At the end of the hour, after the IAD guy and the Chief had left, his decision was made.

"I quit, Brent."

"You can't quit—"

"I just did." Alex leaned forward in the chair, resting his elbows on his knees. "I'll stay for a couple of weeks, long enough to finish my outstanding paper-work, wrap up the Ramos case and transfer my other ones. Then I'm gone.''

From behind the desk, Brent gave him a calculating look. "You'll be back here in three months, tops, begging me for a new assignment."

Alex shook his head. "Not this time. I've had it."

"I can't believe you're quitting." Brent's expression was incredulous. "You're going to miss it, I'm telling you. How can you live without the rush of undercover work?"

He crossed his arms, his voice hard and determined. "That's not living, not anymore. I've been at this for so long, I wake up in the morning not knowing if I'm Alex Worth or Andy Ruiz or Nicholas Alexander—"

"You're a good agent. You've taken some foolish chances but I'd even go so far as to say you're a great one. Are you sure you want to give it all up?"

His mouth flattened in a thin-lipped smile. "Oh, yeah. I'm going to miss lying, cheating, stealing, sleeping around and all of the other things I did for the Special Operations Division."

Brent cocked one eyebrow and spread his hands, both palms upturned. "It's a glamorous job, what can I say?"

"I could easily do without getting 'arrested' again. Dave Sandalis should have been written up for claiming I resisted."

"He's got plenty of bruises to prove you resisted."

Alex scowled. "Only after he slammed me into the wall—"

Brent shrugged. "Hey, you know the drill. It had to look good in front of the other criminals."

"I don't know how well it worked. Ramos knows that his organization was infiltrated. Since he agreed to a plea bargain in exchange for testimony, it won't take long to finger me for the breach." He sighed and turned his head to stare out the window. "I'm burned out, Brent. That makes a man lose his edge. One more reason for me to get the hell out. From now on, I do what I want, answer only to myself."

"I'm telling you. You're going to miss being an agent. A desk job isn't for you. You just won't be happy without the excitement and the challenge—"

"The only thing I'll miss is our golf games." He stood up and reached across the desk to offer his hand. "And who says those have to stop just because we're not working together?"

Brent stood as well and returned the handshake heartily. "I wish you luck, my friend. You know there's always a place for you here if things don't work out."

He didn't say anything, but Alex knew in his heart he wouldn't return to the Justice Department. He hadn't realized how empty his life was until Meghan came into it, hadn't known how much he needed her until she walked out of it. There was one more role for him to take on—the man worthy of her love.

17

Alex is everything I ever wanted in a man, all that
I've dreamed of and more. He touched me in ways
that changed me forever. He was right about the
magic.

MEGHAN INITIALED the last entry with a heavy heart.
The stiff pages rustled as she closed the lavender paisley book. Her fingers trailed slowly across the rough
textured cover. It was like saying goodbye to an old
friend. Her diaries had given her a way to act out her
dreams without getting hurt, an outlet for the sensuality
she repressed.

But she couldn't escape into fantasy anymore. Not
when she'd found the real thing...and let him go.

She set the diary beside her on the turquoise love
seat and glanced around the lemon-colored living room
of Julie's Miami condominium with a wry smile. It was
typical South Beach style—all glass block and pastel
paint. It was also typical of her sister's bright, sunny
personality.

Meghan stared longingly out the large bay windows
to her left. Julie's condo offered a great view of the
Atlantic Ocean, just blocks away, and she wished she'd
had more time to enjoy it over the past month. How-

ever, she'd already gotten her law school reading list
and assignments. For first-year students, Criminal Law
and Civil Procedure, as well as Property, Torts, and
Legal Research were mandatory classes. And she still
had to find a job. She leaned over to push the play
button on the answering machine.

"Hi, Meghan. This is Lisa at Permanent Employment. I'm trying to set up an interview for you. A company called January Investigations, Inc. is looking to
hire someone with a paralegal background. Give me a
call."

She jotted down the time and telephone number.
She'd get in touch with Julie's friend at the agency first
thing in the morning. *Please let something come of this.*
It was hard to find a job that would accommodate her
school schedule, yet pay more than minimum wage.

The next message began to play. "Megs! It's Jules.
Go get a copy of today's paper! You have to read this
article. Talk to you later. 'Bye.''

A telemarketing call followed, then some salesman
offered her an unbeatable rate on a second mortgage.
The last call was a wrong number. None of the mes-
sages were from Alex.

When she'd first returned to Miami, he had called
her to say how much he loved and missed her. He
explained that he'd be unavailable until after he testi-
fied before a grand jury. She hadn't heard from him
since. Too often she found herself wondering where he
was, worrying about what he might be doing.

As busy as her new life kept her, she still had too
much time to think about Alex. Each thought brought
a sharp, stabbing pain through her chest, leaving her

on the verge of tears. The nights were long and lonely without him. The days weren't much better.

Enough. Meghan pushed herself off the love seat. She needed to get out, get some fresh air. Besides, the urgency in Julie's voice aroused her curiosity. She grabbed her purse and door keys and headed for 13th Street. She turned onto Ocean Drive, the heart of the Art Deco district in "SoBe," as Julie referred to the area. She found a newsstand and bought a copy of the *Miami Herald*.

Meghan gasped. Her hands trembled as she read every detail of the front-page article.

DEA Administrator D.R. Marshall announced today the successful conclusion of a two-year investigation, "Operation Dinero." Indictments against seventeen defendants were returned by a federal grand jury for a multimillion-dollar drug profit money-laundering scheme.

Her eyes skimmed down the page, then widened in recognition when she reached the last paragraph.

Most notable was the capture of Francisco Guillermo Ramos by unnamed DEA agents at the exclusive Florida Keys Cayo Sueño resort. Additionally, over 100 million dollars' worth of laundered drug proceeds was seized from Miami-based businesses and financial institutions held by the defendants.

Marshall is quoted as saying, "It is the enormous profits gained from trafficking that fuels the drug trade. We were able to hit the cartel where it hurts, in their pockets. The war on drugs continues, but maybe the work of these brave agents will help to stem the tide.''

Meghan finished reading the article, surprised by the surge of pride she felt. She hated Alex's job and the jeopardy it placed him in, but he was doing what he believed was right.

She'd thought she didn't need any more heroes in her life, but she was wrong. Maybe that's exactly what she needed.

TWO DAYS LATER, she stepped out of the cab and glanced at her watch. She'd been so worried about being late for her interview that she was actually twenty minutes early. Not that she was desperate or anything. Eager, that was it. Eager. This job had everything she needed—flexible hours, benefits and good pay. The way Lisa described the position, it was almost too good to be true.

What would she have to do to get such a perfect job, anyway? Sleep with the boss? Her mind raced from desperate to eager to worried and back. Her stomach went along for the ride. Checking her reflection in the glass door, she wondered if the cherry-red silk camisole and matching heels had been the right choice. Maybe she should have worn something more reserved....

She shrugged. She wasn't the same woman she once was, so why wear the same old clothes? She smoothed one palm over her cream-colored linen suit, ironing out invisible wrinkles. Slipping her hand into the pocket, she closed her fingers around the silver coin Alex had given her, and rubbed it for luck.

Alex. She closed her eyes briefly, torturing herself with the image of his face. His easy laugh and tender hugs, his laid-back charm and passionate kisses. Swallowing hard against the lump in her throat, she went inside and took the elevator to the eleventh floor. A polished brass wall sign pointed the way to January Investigations.

A perky brunette sat behind the reception desk answering telephone calls. A name plate on the desk read "Tiffnee." The moniker perfectly suited the girl's large blue eyes, button nose and rosebud lips. She was really too cute to live.

"Hi! Can I help you?"

I seriously doubt it, Tiffnee. She stared at the girl's mouthful of bubble gum as she introduced herself. "My name is Meghan Foster. I have a ten o'clock appointment with the owner."

The girl's bright expression dimmed by a few degrees. "Aw, man. Like, I'm sorry, but he's not here."

"I'm sure the interview was scheduled for today." Brows furrowed, Meghan checked the date and time Lisa from Permanent Employment had given her.

"Oh, yeah, it is. But, like, the boss had a meeting on Fisher Island. Some kinda security deal for one of the resorts. He should be back soon, though." The girl smiled reassuringly and bobbed her head, causing her dark ringlets to bounce.

Tiffnee even had perky hair. Meghan agreed to wait, but declined the offer of coffee, tea or "this totally cool seaweed drink." As she picked up the phone and started giggling about some boy she'd met at a nightclub, Meghan took a seat in one of the comfortable, overstuffed armchairs and glanced around.

Tiffnee didn't fit the office image at all. Gray marble floor tiles gleamed under the light of etched-glass halogen lamps. Original oils and watercolors graced the walls, which were papered in shell-pink silk. She'd bet the receptionist had played no part in the decorating.

Meghan settled in for a long wait. She crossed her legs, uncrossed them, then crossed them the other way and picked up a magazine. When the front door opened, she glanced up from the copy of *Architectural Digest* she'd been skimming. Tiffnee quickly hung up the phone and sat at attention as a well-dressed man entered the suite.

She could only see him from behind, but he was a walking billboard for success. His dove-gray suit appeared tailor-made for his broad shoulders and confident stride. He carried an expensive-looking leather attaché case, which he set on the desktop. The receptionist greeted him with a megawatt grin, the huge wad of bright pink bubble gum somehow out of sight.

"Hey, boss! Your ten o'clock is here."

The man turned toward Meghan and the magazine dropped out of her numb fingers, landing on the tile floor with a slap. Omigod! Her heart stuttered, then leapt with joy and pounded in her chest. Tears stung her eyes. She couldn't breathe. The world spun faster— or maybe it was her head.

Alex.

And yet she hardly recognized him without the unkempt hair, beard stubble and earring. He stepped forward, not at all surprised to see her. He gave her the friendly-sexy grin that always made her pulse race. "Hello, Trouble."

Hello, Mr. Fabulous.

He was clean-shaven, his hair cut conservatively short, and he was dressed like a normal human being. The only wild floral patterns in sight graced his tie. His boots had been replaced with Italian leather loafers. If possible, he looked even more gorgeous than last time she saw him.

"I can't believe it's you. What are you doing here, Alex?"

Tiffnee chimed in helpfully. "He, like, owns the place."

He was the owner? When did that happen? Maybe he was working undercover again. Maybe this was part of another DEA case. Confused and unsure of how to react, she adjusted her glasses and stood up to greet him.

Should she hug him, kiss him or what? She started to offer her hand, then dropped it to her side. The gesture was ridiculous after the intimacies they'd shared. Alex seemed as uncertain of what to do as she. He reached out to touch her, then hesitated and waved behind him instead.

"Why don't you come back to my office?"

"She's even prettier than you said, boss."

"Excuse me?" Startled, Meghan turned back to look at the receptionist.

Tiffnee winked broadly. "Should I, like, hold your calls while you 'interview' her?"

"Back to work, brat. At least until I fire you."

"Yeah, right. As if." The girl acted completely indifferent to the threat as she picked up an incoming phone call.

"Sorry about that. I promised my uncle I'd give her a job." Alex grinned. "He's my main investor."

He led Meghan along a wide, brightly lit corridor with offices on either side. She followed, still dazed by the extreme difference in his appearance. He showed her into a large corner office with thick gray carpet and large windows overlooking the city. The bold floral pattern of the draperies reminded her of his resort shirts.

Meghan perched stiffly on the edge of the leather couch, setting her briefcase on the floor. "Where have you been, Alex? Is this company really yours? What—?"

"One question at a time." He quirked a brow and smiled when he caught her staring at his leather dress shoes. "I've made a couple of changes."

She sat back against the couch. It took enormous effort to mask her pleasure at seeing him again. All she wanted was to throw herself into his arms and never let go. She wanted to kiss him like crazy and make him promise... *Slow down, Megs,* she stopped herself. *First you need to figure out what's going on.*

"Let's start with the most important question, then. What am I doing here?"

"Julie and Lisa helped me set this up."

Well, now she knew why the job seemed too perfect. He removed his suit jacket and sat down beside her, crossing one ankle over the opposite knee. "The firm needs an office manager so I can go out and develop new clients."

Not exactly the answer she was hoping for. She dropped her gaze to hide the hurt. Disappointment settled painfully into her chest.

"I thought..." Her voice sounded strained, even to

her own ears. She cleared her throat. "I thought maybe you wanted to see me again."

"I did. I do! Absolutely. But I know you'll never commit to being with a cop. So—"

"Tell me about your company. Why did you name it January Investigations?" If the only way she could see Alex was to take this job, then that would have to be enough. She clamped down on her turbulent emotions. She'd deal with the sense of rejection and loss when she could be alone. It looked like she'd be alone for a long time.

"In Roman mythology, Janus is the god of beginnings. He's got a two-headed image, one looking to the past and the other facing the future." He shrugged matter-of-factly. "I thought it was a good name for a man trying to start his life over."

Don't ask, Megs. You could get seriously hurt. Don't even think about it. Don't— "I have to ask. Is there a place for me in your new life?"

His foot hit the floor with a thump when he surged toward her, an earnest expression on his handsome face. "I thought the biggest obstacle between us was my job. Am I wrong?"

"You're wrong." She reached out to clasp his hand, her fingers tightening with the urgency to convey her feelings. The spark was still there, the familiar heat as the pleasure of his touch spread throughout her body. "*I* was wrong. I let stupid, superficial things blind me to the truth."

"What truth is that?" Deep emotions shifted in the kaleidoscope of his light green eyes. His expression was one of cautious hope and she felt the fine tremors in the hand she held. That unexpected nervousness encouraged her to go on.

"The job you do shaped the person you are. Your courage and loyalty and determination are as much a part of you as the color of your hair. I respect and admire those qualities in you. I was wrong to want you to change. I wouldn't have you any other way."

"You have no idea what it means to hear you say that." An odd smile tugged at the corners of his mouth. She watched the play of emotions on his face, saw the love she felt reflected in his gaze.

"I got scared, really scared, when faced with the reality of your job. It terrified me to realize that the one night I experienced is what you face every night." Meghan paused, unable to speak as her voice filled with tears. "So I ran. And turned my back on the one thing I wanted most—your love. Then I read a newspaper article about the Ramos case. I was so proud of you and what you'd accomplished. It made me finally realize that your job doesn't matter—"

His quick, rumbling chuckle startled her. A few locks of dark hair fell forward to brush his temples when he dropped his chin and shook his head. Her brow furrowed as she stared at him. Here she was confessing her deepest feelings and he was laughing at her. "What?"

"You won't believe this, sweetheart. Talk about irony. I quit the DEA. I'm no longer an agent."

"What!"

Surprise and excitement made her pulse race. A future with him suddenly seemed possible. Guilt pricked at her conscience over her joyous reaction, but now he'd be out of danger. As hard as it was to walk away, losing him again would destroy her.

"This is awfully sudden, isn't it?"

"Yeah, I know." He reached up to pinch his left earlobe, obviously not yet accustomed to being without an earring. "The things you said to me, the questions you asked, made me reassess my profession."

"You quit for me?" Her forehead creased into a frown. She wasn't sure she liked the burden of responsibility that entailed. If he regretted the choice later, he might blame her.

"No. I quit for me." Alex's smoke-roughened voice held a firm resolve. "I'd been lying for so long, I couldn't tell the truth when it counted. Working undercover was so ingrained, so natural, I didn't know who I was anymore. I just know I don't like the person I'd become."

Meghan slipped her hand away, not wanting the welcome distraction of his touch just now. "So you traded a badge for a license. You're a man who thrives on challenge, the thrill of the chase. What happens when you change your mind?"

"I won't change it. This is strictly a desk job, Meghan. Arranging for personal security, doing background checks and stuff like that. I don't work the streets anymore."

She studied his face, looking for signs of remorse. "It can't have been easy, giving up your career after so many years. Are you sure about this?"

"It was a lot easier than I thought." Alex stared at the floor, his expression withdrawn and solemn. "I joined the DEA to get even for my little brother. Since you left me, I've had time to re-evaluate my life. I've had to accept that arresting every drug dealer in the world won't bring Greg back. I can't save him, wherever he is.''

She reached out to stroke his face, trying to erase the lines of pain etched around his eyes. He may have cut his hair, shaved and put on a suit, but underneath he was the same man she'd fallen in love with. With Alex she'd found what she was searching for, what she'd longed for in page after page of her diary.

"I love you, whatever your name is." She saw his quick grin in relief. She'd managed to lighten his mood. "You walked out of my fantasies and into my life, and made my dreams come true. I don't care what you do for a living as long as you're living with me."

Alex closed his eyes briefly, too overcome to speak. He'd gone through hell this past month, wanting to call her, see her, hold her in his arms. But he had to get his life in order before he asked her to be a part of it again.

Being with her, it was as if time stopped, as if they'd never parted. Whenever he got near her, he felt the emotional connection, one of tenderness, intimacy and love. She'd unlocked his heart with her quiet beauty, sensuality and courage.

His eyes roamed over her, admiring the changes. Her hair was highlighted and styled in soft curls. Smoky color lined her eyes and deep red lipstick made her lush mouth ripe for kissing. The skirt of her suit was short, form-fitting and very sexy. A familiar hunger, wild and demanding, grew inside him. Cupping her cheek, he leaned down, intending to kiss her.

"There's just one more thing I want to know." Meghan's hand on his chest stopped him. So did the serious tone of her voice and the intensity of her gaze. "Did you read my whole diary?"

Hell, without even trying he could recall whole passages of the most erotic words he'd ever read. He thought they'd gotten past this, but apparently it was still an issue. He braced himself for whatever her reaction might be. "Yeah. I did."

She gave him a teasingly provocative smile. "Then we have some more fantasies to act out, don't we?"

He smiled back. "A lot more. I haven't told you any of mine. And I hope you'll fulfill one for me now."

Alex got down on one knee in front of her and reached into his trouser pocket. He opened the ring box to reveal a one-carat emerald flanked by diamonds in an antique gold setting. She gasped and her hands clapped over her mouth.

"You take my breath away. With a look, the slightest touch, the sweetness of your smile. You're everything good in my life. I can't go on without you. Marry me, Trouble. Share my life and make it whole. Make *me* whole. Be mine, and let me be yours."

She knelt down before him, taking his hands in hers. Tears spilled down her cheeks and he felt his own eyes well up. Her voice was husky with emotion. "I love you, Alex. With all my heart, I love you. You're the best thing that ever happened to me. You complete me. There's nothing I want more than to spend forever with you."

Chest aching with the power of his joy, he slid the ring onto her finger. Meghan smiled and reached for him. Her fingers skimmed his brow, touched his cheeks, traced the contours of his mouth. She put her hands on either side of his face and pulled him forward until their lips met.

The kiss was warm, sweet and heartbreakingly tender. Alex savored the softness of her lips, the faint peppermint taste of her mouth, the eagerness of her response. She opened to him, sliding her tongue over his in slow exploration. Desire sang in his blood as she combed her fingers through his hair and deepened the kiss.

He wrapped his arms around her waist, reveled in the feel of her soft breasts on his chest. His hands glided down her back to squeeze her round, firm butt. Meghan undid his tie, eyeing it as she slid it from his collar. "That's a very interesting pattern. Did you cut up one of your shirts or have extra fabric from the drapes?"

Alex grinned down at her. "I bought it with you in mind."

He slipped her suit jacket from her shoulders, his fingers gliding over the bare skin of her upper arms. Her skin warmed beneath his roving hands. Then he saw it—the price she'd paid for loving him. He gently brushed his lips over the shiny pink scar on top of her right shoulder in silent apology.

She met his gaze with a gentle smile. "It's okay, Alex. It will remind us never to take what we have for granted."

She unbuttoned his shirt, kissing his jaw, the base of his throat and then his bare chest. Heart racing, he reached around to unzip her skirt, letting it pool around her knees. He kissed her wildly, passionately. Their arms tangled when he tried to unfasten her camisole while she attempted to tug off his shirt.

"This isn't working." Meghan laughed as he took his shirt off himself and she pulled the camisole over her head. Alex got to his feet, helping her up at the same time. He led her over to his desk and punched a button on the telephone without releasing her hand.

"Tiffnee, hold my calls for the next hour."

As the receptionist babbled on about his appointments for the day, he looked at Meghan. She stood beside him wearing only a red bra, lace panties and her cherry-red high-heeled pumps. He thought back to that first day at Cayo Sueño, to his wish of seeing her in the red lingerie and "seduce me" sandals.

Her eyes boldly traveled over his body and he felt the heat of her gaze like a physical touch. Sexual heat flared between them as she licked her lips mischievously. Then she leaned over to gently take his nipple into her mouth. He struggled not to groan aloud. She reached for his belt buckle while kissing a hot, wet path from his chest and down his torso toward—

"Make that the rest of the afternoon, Tiffnee."

He hung up the phone and pulled Meghan to her feet. In the space of a breath, he found her lips again. As his tongue teased her mouth open in an urgent and demanding kiss, her hands caressed his bare back. He unhooked her bra and cupped the warm weight of her breasts in his palms.

When Meghan broke the kiss and began to step out of her shoes, he stopped her. "Leave those on, Trouble. They're a reminder of the way we met. Besides, you won't be on your feet for long."

"That desk doesn't look very comfortable."

"The sofa pulls out into a double bed. Let's play the Horny Boss and the Delectable Secretary."

Her laugh was low and throaty. "Oh, Alex. You and your theme games."

Saturday, October 5

She is one hot babe. Gorgeous, smart, sexy as hell. And at the moment, completely at my mercy. She strains against the silk ropes binding her wrists to the bedpost. But the excited gleam in her eyes gives her away....

ALEX WAS GOING TO ENJOY Meghan's reaction when she read his entry. He was eager to act out this fantasy during their honeymoon, but right now he had to get dressed for the wedding. He closed the journal with a grin. Yeah. Reality beat fantasy every time.

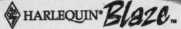

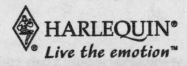

If you enjoyed what you just read,
then we've got an offer you can't resist!

Take 2 bestselling
love stories FREE!
Plus get a FREE surprise gift!

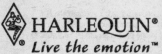
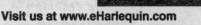